The Girls' Gang

Mr Mills had always enjoyed taking Year 6. He liked the way you knew where you were with eleven-year-olds. By this stage, they'd been pretty well moulded into shape. But this group of girls was different. It wasn't that they were badly behaved or refused to get their work done; it was the fact that they wouldn't keep quiet and leave him alone. They were so persistent. They were forever coming up with some new scheme to disrupt the class, and they wouldn't just do the jobs they were given. They always had to have a half-hour discussion about whether it was fair or not. Fair! Whoever pretended that schools were fair?

Also by Rose Impey

Fireballs From Hell

THE
GIRLS' GANG

ROSE IMPEY

With illustrations by Colin Meir

Collins
An Imprint of HarperCollinsPublishers

For Kate and Lynne

First published in Great Britain in 1986 by
William Heinemann Ltd.
First published in Lions in 1989
This edition published by Collins in 1996
1 3 5 7 9 8 6 4 2

Collins is an imprint of
HarperCollins*Publishers* Ltd.,
77-85 Fulham Palace Road,
Hammersmith, London W6 8JB.

Printed and bound in Great Britain by
HarperCollins Manufactuing, Glasgow

CONTENTS

INTRODUCING
THE GANG

It's Sandra who suggests having a gang – she's the dramatic one – although really it was Jane's idea. But she's used to her sister taking the limelight. It's Cheryl who gets them properly organized – she's the clever one. Jo wants to be in the gang but filling in membership cards is too much like school for her liking. Louise thinks it's all very exciting but worrying too – she doesn't like being in trouble. And the main thing about The Girls' Gang is that trouble seems to come looking for them.

THE GIRLS' GANG MEMBERSHIP CARD

★☆★☆★☆★☆★☆★☆★☆★☆★☆★☆★

NAME Sandra Turner.

ADDRESS 58, Broadway Rd, Witton, England, The World, The Universe.

AGE 10 years, 4 months 1 week 3 days 2 hours 12 minutes.

HEIGHT 1 m. 50 cm.

WEIGHT 35 Kg.

INTERESTS Acting, Reading, The Gang, Films on T.V.

AMBITIONS To be the most famous actress in the world.

LIKES 1. Plays 2. Reading in bed 3. Sweets.

DISLIKES 1. Games 2. assemblies 3. school dinners.

THE GIRLS' GANG MEMBERSHIP CARD

NAME Jane Turner

ADDRESS 58 Broadway Rd Wilton

AGE 10 years 4 months 1 week 3 days 2 hours 10 minutes

HEIGHT 1m 50cm

WEIGHT 34kg

INTERESTS Plays - Gymnastics - T.V. and the Gang

AMBITIONS To be a Famous Gymnast - not to be a Twin.

LIKES 1. Gymnastics 2. Reading in the bath 3. Shopping

DISLIKES 1. Being told what to do 2. Being a twin 3. Soggy Books

THE GIRLS' GANG MEMBERSHIP CARD

NAME Cheryl Spencer

ADDRESS 15, Highway Road, Wilton

AGE 10 years 9 months

HEIGHT 1m. 56cm.

WEIGHT 40 kg

INTERESTS 1. Experiments, Chess, Thinking, Plays and Eating.

AMBITIONS To be a famous scientist like Einstein or David Bellamy

LIKES 1. Science Fiction Stories. 2. Pizza 3 Maths

DISLIKES 1. Boys 2. Going to bed 3. Getting up.

THE GIRLS' GANG MEMBERSHIP CARD

☆★☆★☆★☆★☆★☆★☆★☆★☆★☆★☆★☆

NAME Jo Robson

ADDRESS 12 Weaver Way, Witton

AGE 10 years 3 months,

HEIGHT 1m 38cm

WEIGHT 30 kg.

INTERESTS Jimnastics - football and other Sports

AMBITIONS to win a few gold meddles at the next Olympics

LIKES 1. running 2. being in a gang 3. Lynford Christie

DISLIKES 1. School 2. boys 3. speling tests.

THE GIRLS' GANG MEMBERSHIP CARD

☆★☆★☆★☆★☆★☆★☆★☆★☆★☆★☆★☆

NAME Louise Bottomley

ADDRESS The Dell, Tinkers Close, Witton

AGE 11 years 1 week

HEIGHT 1m 51cms

WEIGHT 37 kg.

INTERESTS Pop music and clothes and T.V.

AMBITIONS To be an air-hostess or pop singer

LIKES 1. Take That. 2. Beefburgers 3. Dancing

DISLIKES 1. Having my hair cut 2. Looking after my sister.

THE NEW GIRLS

It was the first day back at Witton Park Primary School after the long summer holiday. Mr Mills sat at his desk. He watched his new Year 6 class as they began writing in their spotless exercise books.

"I want you to write about yourselves," he had said, "your likes and dislikes, interests, ambitions, weaknesses, anything you want to tell me."

"Weaknesses, Sir?" said Ralph Raven. "I can't think of any off hand." The girls could have given Ralph a few suggestions. He had only been in the class a couple of hours and Mr Mills could already think of one or two himself.

"I'm sure you'll think of something, Ralph," he said. "Now, make a start. I want at least a couple of pages before lunch-time."

Some of the class had groaned. Any kind of writing was hard work as far as they were concerned. But most people had felt relieved. At least they didn't have to write about "My Holidays".

On the way to school Cheryl had been dreading the possibility. "I've had to write about 'My Holidays' in every class I've been in," she said to Jo. "It's the worst thing about coming back to school."

"When my brother started at the High School," said Jo, "they had to do it four times on the first day. In English, Humanities, French and Music. I mean, what have holidays got to do with music?"

Cheryl Spencer and Jo Robson often walked to school together. They were both odd-ones-out in the class, but they seemed to be able to put up with each other's differences. Cheryl was the tallest girl in the school and everyone called her a "boff". She wrote in her book:

"When I grow up I intend to be a famous scientist like Einstein or David Bellamy. I shall discover things like gravity and rare snakes. I might even be a nuclear physicist, except I don't approve of bombs."

Jo was the smallest person in the class, but she was fast and athletic. She was not very good at school work. She couldn't seem to sit still long enough to learn anything.

"I have four older bruthers," she wrote, "and they make me sik. They sit on me and pinch my sweets and leeve me owt. I downt think its faire that boys are biger than grils somethink ort to be done abowt it."

Across the table from them sat Louise Bottomley. She was a shy girl, with long blonde hair and dreamy eyes. Sometimes she had friends; other times she was left on her own. Today she sat opposite Cheryl, next to the new girls.

"I hate people calling me 'Knickers', just because my name's Bottomley," she wrote, "or 'Bumley', which is worse. I wish they wouldn't do it. It hurts my feelings."

Mr Mills looked around the room. He picked out one or two individuals whose reputations had travelled ahead of them. Ralph Raven. He was considered to be the loudest boy they'd had in the school for many years, probably since it opened. Stuart Harvey. He was certainly the greediest. He wasn't a fat boy, but he deserved to be. He was the only person who had school dinners *and* brought a packed lunch as well. Cheryl Spencer. She was probably the cleverest girl they'd had since her sister left five years ago. And Jo Robson could sometimes be the most awkward. She wore a permanent frown, some small complaint always on her lips. And then these two new girls were an unknown quantity. The message Mr Mills had received from their last school had troubled him. It simply said, "Watch those Turner twins!"

Mr Mills was short of furniture and Sandra and Jane Turner were squeezed on to the corner of Cheryl's table. Sandra was holding her forehead and gazing out of the window for inspiration. She had already written two sides. Jane was stuck after half a page. She leaned over to read her sister's work, to get some ideas.

"I shall be a world-famous actress when I leave school," Sandra had written. "I have had several star parts already. My last teacher said that I have a rich imagination, which is why I'm so good at acting."

"That's a fat lie," said Jane. "What she said was, 'You live in a dream world most of the time and the rest of the time you're showing off.'"

"Why do you have to make everything sound dull and boring?" said Sandra.

Their mother could never understand how they could be so different and yet look so alike. Although Jane was dark and Sandra was fair, they were clearly twins. One was like the negative of the other. What a pleasant, easy child they would have made, she thought, if only they had been one instead of two.

Sandra had enough wild ideas and fantasies for both of them, while Jane had all the common sense.

At their old school everyone had been perfectly used to them. The novelty of them being twins had worn off in Year 1. Changing schools meant they were going to have to go through the fuss all over again. Jane hated being stared at, as if they each had two heads or had recently landed from another planet, but Sandra loved the attention. She never missed an opportunity to show off. She put on silly faces and false voices, until Jane felt really embarrassed. It was like when your mother meets someone in the street, and talks in a posh voice you don't recognize, and you want to crawl through the grating and disappear down the drain. Jane often felt like this.

She wrote in her exercise book, "Sometimes, I wish I was shipwrecked on a desert island – ALONE. There would be no boat and no wood to make a raft, no bottles to put messages in and, most of all, no sister with me!"

Cheryl looked up from her writing and studied the new girls, as if they were rare specimens. She made a hobby of watching people. It didn't matter how awful they were, you could find something of interest, if you watched closely enough. Even Ralph Raven provided hours of useful observation. In a way he was so appalling, he was fascinating. Cheryl thought Sandra was a most unusual character. Jo thought she was plain stupid and wished she'd go and sit somewhere else. Louise thought she was wonderful, but was far too shy to speak to her.

Mr Mills looked over and noticed, not for the first time, how the odd-balls in a class always seemed to be drawn together, like magnets. Look at Ralph Raven and Stuart Harvey, partners in crime. He would have to watch those two very carefully. Thank goodness the group of girls was unlikely to cause him as much concern. He'd never had any real trouble with girls – in the past.

After lunch, Mr Mills corrected spelling mistakes and asked the class to write out their work neatly for a wall display.

"What a waste of time," said Jo, who was a slow writer. "We could have written it on paper in the first place."

"It's so you get rid of your mistakes," said Louise, decorating her work with a border of flowers and birds and butterflies.

"What mistakes?" said Jo, as she wrote, "Abowt miself."

While they were writing, Ralph Raven wandered over to the girls' table. He often prowled the classroom when he felt in need of a little entertainment.

He perched on the only spare corner of the table and said,

"What's it like, being twins?"

"What d'you mean, what's it like? That's a daft question," said Jane.

"What's it like being an idiot?" Cheryl asked him.

"Nobody asked you to butt in," said Ralph, clipping Cheryl's ear. "I mean," he went on, "it must be pretty awful, having two like you around all the time."

"It'd be pretty horrific, having two like you around any of the time," said Jo. She wrote her last word and carefully remembered the full stop. Ralph leaned over and nudged her arm, so that the full stop continued right up the page. It put a neat line through everything she had written so far. "Aw, look what you've done, you toad," said Jo. "Now I'll have to do it again."

Ralph read Sandra's writing over her shoulder.

"I shall be a world-famous actress when I leave school," he read in a high voice. Sandra covered her work with her arms.

"You have to be good-looking for that," he said, "unless you're going to work in horror movies." Sandra clenched her fists.

"Clear off," said Jane. She could see trouble brewing.

"Make me," said Ralph.

"Ralph Raven, sit down for goodness' sake," said Mr Mills. "Now, hurry up and finish your writing. I want to choose some class monitors before home-time."

Next Mr Mills gave his new class a serious talking to, about what he expected from them now they were in Year 6. Most of the class realized, within minutes, that it was the same "serious talking to" they'd had in every other class they'd been in. So they kept themselves occupied scratching their names on table legs, or picking scabs on their knees, or plaiting their hair and sucking it. At last, seeing a number of glazed eyes, Mr Mills brought his talk to an end. Then he asked for volunteers for the various jobs and responsibilities in the class: mixing the paints, cleaning out the classroom pets and keeping his stock-cupboard tidy. This last job was no easy matter. Mr Mills was the untidiest teacher in the school, probably the entire country, if such a competition could ever be devised. His stock cupboard was overflowing with all sorts of rubbish, which rushed out whenever you opened the door as if desperate to get away. It had become a myth in the school and was used to frighten the infants. "Do as I tell ya or I'll lock ya in Mr Mills' cupboard," little five-year-olds were told and then went crying to the dinner ladies.

Of course, there are some jobs which are more sought after. These involve very little work, but carry the added bonus of getting you out of class time. Collecting sandwich trays throughout the school and stacking them in the Hall was a popular job. People had been known to fight over it. This job traditionally fell to the boys because the trays were said to be heavy. So when Mr Mills asked for volunteers several hands shot up and boys all over the classroom leapt out of their seats.

"Me, Sir! . . . Sir, me!" they shouted.

Ralph Raven drew himself up to his full height and glared at the other boys. One by one they dropped their hands miserably to their sides. Ralph grinned. But then, to his horror, Sandra gripped Jane's hand and raised both their arms in the air.

"We'll do it, Sir," she said. "We're very reliable."

Everyone was shocked. This was a serious matter.

"Don't be stupid," said Ralph. "It's a boys' job. Them trays are 'eavy. Girls'll never lift 'em, Sir, honest."

"I think Ralph's right," said Mr Mills. "We'll leave that job to the boys."

"Why?" asked Sandra.

Mr Mills was flustered for a moment. He wasn't used to girls questioning his authority. Really, there was no good reason, except that it was the way things always were in his class. Mr Mills was a teacher of habit. But the determined look on Sandra's face made him stop and consider. He couldn't stand a long, drawn-out discussion, not on the first day of term.

"Oh, very well," he said. "You two girls can do it for a few weeks. We'll give someone else a chance later."

Ralph Raven looked at the twins as if they had just crawled out of the woodwork and he would like to have trodden on them. Sandra returned the look with a smile, both sweet and sickly.

At home-time, Sandra and Jane walked past the Library towards the allotments. The path through them provided a useful short-cut to their new home. A little way ahead Ralph Raven and Stuart Harvey were waiting, by the allotment gates. They grabbed a girl each and began to shake them, like two dogs shaking a pair of rats.

"Now, listen here, you little creeps," said Ralph Raven, "you can't come to our school and start throwing your weight around. We don't like bossy girls in our class, do we, 'Arvey?" And he shook Sandra hard.

"No, we don't like bossy girls, do we, Raven?" said Stuart Harvey, shaking Jane harder.

"Get lost, you great ape," said Sandra, making

Ralph even more angry. Jane had the good sense to say nothing, but Sandra never knew when to keep quiet.

Just then, Jo and Cheryl were walking home together. Louise was tagging along beside them.

"What do you think of those twins?" asked Cheryl.

"Not much," said Jo. "That Sandra's posh."

This was one of the worst insults Jo could think of. You didn't have to be rich or speak well to be called "posh", you just had to be different.

"I think she's fascinating," said Cheryl.

"Yes, but then you find slugs fascinating," said Jo.

"Oh, look, there they are," said Louise. "Ralph Raven's beating them up."

Despite her opinion of Sandra, Jo raced over to help. She began kicking Ralph's ankles. Cheryl came up behind him and put her hands tightly over his eyes, while Louise grabbed handfuls of hair and tried to pull it out. Stuart Harvey soon disappeared, leaving Ralph to fend off all five girls. At last he, too, escaped. He was hot and cross. He couldn't ever remember being set on by girls before. Five against one hardly seemed fair to him.

"It's a good job you lot came along," said Jane.

Sandra picked up her dinner-bag. There was the tinkling sound of a broken flask.

"The great oaf," she said.

"He's a coward really,' said Cheryl. "He only picks on people smaller than himself."

"Trouble is, most of us are," said Jo.

"My mum says you're better ignoring Ralph Raven," said Louise.

"There are some things you can't ignore," said Cheryl, "and Ralph Raven shaking you to death is one of them."

The girls sat on the allotment gates. Louise handed round a packet of crisps left from dinner-time.

"I hate Ralph Raven," said Jo.

"I hate boys full stop," said Sandra.

"They always get their own way," said Jane.

"It's because they're bigger than us," said Louise.

"But we showed them just now," said Jo, grinning.

"There isn't anything girls can't do, if they stick together," Cheryl told them.

"Yeah," said Jane, "girls ought'a stick together."

They all ate crisps while they considered this idea.

"Why don't we have a gang?" said Sandra, "the five of us. That could be the password."

"What could?"

"Girls ought'a stick together."

"It's a bit long for a password," said Cheryl.

They tried to come up with something better.

"What about 'Ghost'?" said Jo, pleased with herself.

"Ghost?" The other girls looked puzzled.

"You take the first letters, G-O-S-T. Girls-Ought'a-Stick-Together."

"What happened to the 'H'?" said Sandra. "There's an 'H' in ghost, stupid! Can't you spell?"

Jo was a hopeless speller and she knew it, but she didn't want this posh, new girl calling her "stupid".

"OK, Clever Clogs. What about Girls-Had-Ought'a-Stick-Together?" Jo was hopeless at English too.

"Oh, honestly," said Sandra, in disgust. She didn't look as if she wanted to be in a gang with someone who couldn't spell.

"I think it's a good idea," said Cheryl. "We could call ourselves 'The Girls' Gang'."

"Great!" said Jane.

The girls joined right hands and made a promise: "To stick together, whatever happened". That way, they could stand up to some of the boys in their class, boys like Ralph Raven and Stuart Harvey. They agreed to meet later, at Cheryl's house, to make plans.

Cheryl lived with her mum and her older sister in a

terraced house. There were three floors and the top floor was one large bedroom-cum-playroom. This was Cheryl's private property. She and her mum had an understanding about it. Jo had called at the house for Cheryl a few times in the past, but she had never really been inside. So all the girls were in for a surprise when Cheryl showed them her bedroom.

It was more like a museum or a second-hand shop. It was full of rubbish. Collections of broken birds' eggs, grubby bits of rock, piles of books and magazines and animal homes covered every surface. The sloping walls were plastered with pictures of animals and insects, sometimes four or five times as large as life. Louise shuddered to think about the kind of nightmares she'd have if she had to look at those before she went to sleep. There were old saucers with bits of unrecognizable food in different stages of decay and something dead and furry was stretched out and pinned to a board on the corner of Cheryl's desk.

Sandra dramatically put her hand over her mouth, as if she might be sick. Jane kicked her. Fortunately, Cheryl didn't notice. Louise was staring open-mouthed around the room. Creepy-crawlies and furry animals terrified her. Just the thought of beetles and spiders made her feel sick.

24

Her mum said Louise had a "sensitive stomach". Jo called her plain mardy.

"Don't stand there, as if you're waiting for a bus," said Cheryl. "Sit down." She handed the others a piece of computer paper each. Her mum brought piles of it home from work. "I think we should have membership cards," she said. "We can work them out in rough first."

Jo groaned. More writing. She'd come to join a gang, not play at a school.

"What have we got to put?" asked Louise.

"Details about yourself. Name and address first," said Cheryl.

"And height and weight," said Jane.

"And interests and ambitions and things," said Sandra.

"I don't think I've got any ambitions," said Jo, not entirely sure what it meant.

"'Course you have," said Sandra. "Everyone's got ambitions, unless they're vegetables."

"Even vegetables might have ambitions," said Cheryl. "We don't really know." The others looked at her as if she was mad.

"Think about what you'd like to do more than anything in the world," said Jane, helpfully.

"Oh, I see what you mean," said Jo. "Like beat up Ralph Raven single-handed and then sit on him."

"No," said Jane. "That's not what I mean."

"What are you good at?" said Sandra. "There must be something, I suppose. Apart from spelling, of course." Jo went red and drew her eyebrows together in a scowl.

"She's brilliant at games," said Cheryl. "She's the fastest girl in the school. She even plays football with the team sometimes." Sandra was not impressed by this. In her opinion, any girl who chose to play anything with the revolting specimens she'd seen in Year 6 must need her head testing.

"Well then," said Jane. "What do you hope to be when you grow up? I want to be a famous gymnast."

Jo considered this. She liked gymnastics too. Under interests she wrote, "jimnastiks footbal and other sprots".

There was a short, comfortable silence while they each thought about what else they wanted to put on their cards. Cheryl looked up and watched the other girls. She was going to enjoy being in a gang. It felt good having friends in her bedroom like this. Sometimes she was tired of being one on her own. Louise was excited and worried at the same time. She wondered whether the other girls might get her into trouble. But this worry didn't seem enough to put her off. The twins were pleased to have made three new friends so quickly. Only Jo had her doubts. She was dead keen on being in a gang, but she still wasn't sure about that big-headed Sandra. Jo thought four would have been a better number for a gang.

As if reading her mind Sandra said:

"I don't think we should let anybody else join this gang, it should be just the five of us."

"Well, five's enough," said Jane.

"Five's more than enough," muttered Jo.

"Let those boys start anything from now on," said Cheryl.

The girls pushed back their sleeves, as if ready for action. They certainly looked like a force to be reckoned with. If Ralph Raven had been a fly on that bedroom wall he would have hibernated for the winter on the spot. And it would have been better for Ralph if he had.

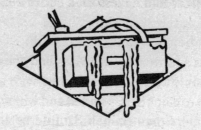

THE FARM VISIT

Over the next few weeks, the five girls went everywhere together. At school they still shared a table, taking it in turns to sit at the corner. Most days, after school, they met at Cheryl's house. They had gang meetings or made up plays or practised gymnastics on Cheryl's bed. The girls tried to keep well away from Ralph Raven. They didn't want any trouble. But Ralph couldn't seem to keep away from them. He was looking for an opportunity to get his own back. He wasn't likely to forget that first day, when those wretched girls had nearly beaten him up. He hung around them, playing stupid practical jokes, which only made the girls angry. In the end this led to a most humiliating defeat for Ralph and one which caused a terrible stink.

"Today I want to talk about the class project we're going to do," said Mr Mills, "on 'Farming'."

Several faces looked less than enthusiastic.

"That's not very exciting," one or two people muttered.

This was exactly why Mr Mills had chosen it. He liked to start off the new school year with a nice safe project. One which he knew well and which wouldn't provide much opportunity for stupid behaviour.

Mr Mills would never forget the one year when he had decided to have a change. He had thought he would do a project on "Water". He had a particularly difficult class that year, and perhaps he should have known better. But he was younger then and less experienced. He had set up a sand tray in his classroom, through which water trickled, making streams and valleys. He closed off the outlet hose by tying a knot in it, which should have been adequate. But there was an especially stupid boy in this class, called Gary Fogerty. In a moment of boredom he had cut through the hose with a pair of craft scissors. He had stood there for a moment sealing the end with his thumb, but he had soon got bored with that. Fearing discovery he had poked the hose into a nearby drawer and wedged it shut. Unfortunately in the drawer were trays of powder paint, six different colours.

During story-time, at the end of the afternoon, Mr Mills suddenly noticed that the class was not listening to him at all. They were watching the set of drawers, beneath the water tray. A multi-coloured froth was pouring out of one of the drawers, like a lurid volcanic eruption. It was travelling slowly but steadily across the classroom floor. No one moved or spoke. The class sat, as if hypnotized. Mr Mills toyed with the idea of reading on, until home-time, to see if they would continue to sit there, while the foam washed over their feet and gradually rose up to drown them all.

Mr Benbow, the caretaker, had never forgotten or forgiven Mr Mills. School caretakers, like elephants, have remarkably long memories. It had also provided Mr Thacker, the headmaster, with a good deal of amusement. He was the sort of person who seems to delight in other people's misfortunes. He stood in Mr Mills' classroom, leaning against a bookcase, shaking with laughter and mopping his face with a handkerchief, while Mr Mills tried to clean it up. You could still see the stains on the floor at the end of the year. So there was no chance that Mr Mills would ever repeat the experiment. Each year now, he took the class out to a local farm. Farming was a good safe subject.

"I have organized two visits to start us off," he

told the class. "One to a cattle-market . . ." Ralph Raven and Stuart Harvey couldn't resist a few "Mooos". ". . . and the other to a local farm. Unlike most modern farms this one still practises mixed farming, so there will be plenty of different animals to see, as well as farm buildings and machinery."

A few of the boys looked more excited at this news. They did mimes of driving tractors at speed round corners with much screeching of brakes. Mr Mills soon put a stop to that and gave the class another serious talking to, about what kind of behaviour he expected from them on these visits. "And most of all," he said, "I don't expect anyone to be unkind to the animals."

This prompted several people in the class to be unkind to one another. They made rude remarks about "some" people going to visit their relatives and told them to be careful they didn't get left behind in the pig-sties. Sometimes Mr Mills wondered why he bothered.

"All right, all right," he said, "that's enough. Now don't forget you'll need wellingtons for both these trips. If there's any mess to be found no doubt you'll all manage to trample through it."

"Sometimes Mr Mills talks to us as if we're a load of infants," Sandra complained.

Jane looked across to where Ralph Raven was stepping into imaginary puddles of sewage. "I'm afraid some of us are," she said.

On Friday morning Year 6 assembled outside the school and then piled on to the coach. Even before the bus started, Stuart Harvey had unpacked his sandwiches and begun eating. They were only going for the morning. They would be back in time for lunch, but it was like an automatic response with him. A bus journey, or anything different from the normal routine, offered a good excuse for a picnic.

"Stuart Harvey, put that food away. Good Heavens, lad, it must be all of an hour since you had your breakfast."

"I thought it seemed a long time, Sir. My stomach was really rumbling."

At the cattle-market, they watched as trailer-loads of animals were herded into pens which looked far too small to hold them. Packed in together, they were a heaving mass of life. They squirmed and wriggled, like tins of maggots, so that you couldn't tell which were their heads and which were their tails. The animal noise was deafening. It made Mr Mills realize there were worse places to work than a primary classroom. The only thing which seemed to rise above the bleats and grunts was the sound of the auctioneer, calling for bids. The volume of his voice was impressive. Several people asked Ralph Raven whether he had considered auctioneering as a job, when he left school. Ralph liked the idea. He listened carefully, trying to pick up a few tips.

Later, Year 6 watched while a pen full of sheep had their ears punched to show they had been to market. It looked painful. It reminded Jo of the time when she had stapled a display label through her finger. She had stood looking, for a moment, at the word "Brontosaurus", wondering whether she had copied it wrongly, before passing out with the pain. Ralph Raven and Stuart Harvey were watching the farmer with their usual morbid interest. They seemed to be getting very friendly with him.

"Perhaps they want him to pierce their ears next," said Cheryl.

"I hope he pierces Ralph Raven's nose while he's about it," said Jo. She had an amusing vision of leading Ralph by the nose around the auctioneer's ring.

When they were all waiting for the bus to take them back to school, Ralph and Stuart came pushing into the girls and generally making a nuisance of themselves. Ralph grabbed Louise's anorak pocket and nearly ripped it off. Mr Mills told the boys to "Get in line" and "Stop showing me up". Both boys looked innocently over their shoulders, as if he were talking to someone else.

Louise felt in her pocket, where she found a soft, squidgy mess. She brought out her hand. In it were the scraps of half a dozen sheep's ears. They lay there, pink and pathetic, making her feel quite depressed. She didn't know what to do with them. It didn't seem right to drop them on the floor, like unwanted litter.

"Oh, give them to me," said Cheryl, "they'll do for my collection." Cheryl picked up all sorts of things: sheep's eyes, cows' tongues, bird skulls. Jane called it "Cheryl's Chamber of Horrors". Just thinking about it gave Louise nightmares. Her mum would have had a screaming fit if she'd ever kept anything like that in her bedroom.

On the way back, in the bus, Ralph decided to practise his auctioneering skills on the girls' gang.

"Who'll give me five? Who'll give me five? Who'll give me five p for this fine, fat heifer?" he said, pointing at Louise.

She blushed, the colour rising like a thermometer.

"Now, what am I bid? What am I bid for these two rare goats, one black, one white," he said, indicating the twins. "ten p for the two and cheap at half the price."

Sandra glared at Ralph, as if aiming two poisonous darts at his head. They bounced off with no effect at all. "And who'll give me two p for this runt pig? The weedy one of the litter, I won't deny it, but give it a good home and it might survive."

Cheryl had to hold Jo down at this point.

"Ignore him," she said, "he's not worth bothering with."

Next it was Cheryl's turn.

"Who can I pay? Who can I pay to take this old carthorse off my hands? Not much life in her but worth a few pence at the glue factory," he said.

Cheryl began to get out of her seat.

"I'll tell you what," he offered the rest of the bus, "I'll do you a deal. Bargain of the week. I don't want a pound. I don't even want a penny. In fact I'll pay you to take 'em."

All five girls looked as if they were about to take Ralph apart and auction the pieces, but Mr Mills stepped in.

"Just sit down and give your voice a rest, will you?"

"But it isn't tired, Sir," said Ralph.

"No, but everyone else is," said Mr Mills.

As they walked home from school that day, the girls were still smarting from Ralph Raven's insults on the bus. Other boys in the class had taken up the idea and had continued to sell off the girls to one another throughout the day at more and more humiliating prices. The joke was wearing very thin indeed.

"Ralph Raven is really looking for trouble," said Jo. She viciously kicked a stone out of her path, as if it were Ralph Raven himself.

"Oh, don't worry about him," said Sandra. "I've got one or two ideas for sorting him out."

"What sort of ideas?" said Jo.

"Oh, that would be telling," said Sandra, smiling.

"You can tell us," said Jo. "We're supposed to be in a gang, aren't we?"

But Sandra only went on smiling and said nothing. This made Jo furious.

"Take no notice," said Jane. "She hasn't any more ideas than us. She's just trying to look clever."

Sandra was embarrassed and this made her spiteful.

"Well, someone in this gang has got to have the ideas," she said. "It's a good job we're not all stupid."

Jo scowled and went off home in a sulk.

"Now look what you've done,' said Jane.

On the following Tuesday morning, Mr Mills warned Ralph Raven and the rest of the class in general that the farm they were to visit belonged to a personal friend of his. He particularly asked them to remember their manners and to try not to do anything silly. Ralph grinned, as if he had been singled out for some special honour. Mr Mills wondered if it was possible to make an impression on Ralph. He was like one of those children's plastic toys – a Mr Wobbly – with a curved base. No matter how often you knock it down, it always springs back up for more.

It was a sunny autumn morning as they walked the mile and a half to the farm. On the way Mr Mills pointed out things of interest. One or two people listened. The rest of them walked in and out of the gutter, determined to overtake one another, as if it was a race. Mr Mills was finding it difficult to keep up with them.

When they arrived, the farmer, Mr Squires, greeted the class. Then he took them on a guided tour. He showed them his herd of Friesian cows and the milking parlour, his small flock of pedigree sheep and his prize-winning pigs. There was a colourful collection of rare-breed poultry: hens with funny hats and cockerels with feathered trousers, strutting around the farmyard.

When they went inside the hen-houses, Ralph Raven and Stuart Harvey lurked quietly at the back. They emerged minutes later, looking guilty. Stuart

Harvey was clutching his hand. One of the hens had pecked him. Mr Mills thought that it probably served him right. Stuart Harvey never could resist the sight of food.

At eleven o'clock, the farmer led them to one of his hay-barns, where there was a drink of squash and a biscuit for each of them. Mr Mills and the farmer leaned on a fence and chatted. The class split into small groups and found seats for themselves on bales of hay. Jane and Sandra went to sit down, balancing a drink in one hand and a biscuit in the other. Ralph and Stuart mysteriously appeared behind them. The twins instinctively ducked their heads.

"Here comes trouble," said Jane. But the boys held out their hands, to show they weren't up to anything.

Turning their backs, the girls sat down. There was a faint cracking sound. They both shot up.

"Oh, look," said Ralph. "They laid an egg."

On the hay were the broken egg shells and down the seat of the girls' jeans ran the slimy mess of egg. It took them the rest of the break-time to wipe themselves clean with dry straw. But the girls still felt uncomfortable, as if they had wet themselves.

Mr Mills didn't notice the girls, but he was always alert to Ralph Raven and Stuart Harvey. They were looking thoroughly pleased with themselves. He could tell they had been up to something.

"All right, what's the joke?"

"Joke, Sir?" said Ralph.

"Something seems to be amusing you two," said Mr Mills.

"It's them girls, Sir, they always make us laugh. I think they're a bit cracked," said Ralph. And he and Stuart rolled around laughing, while Mr Mills looked on puzzled.

Next, Mr Mills drew the class together and the farmer took them on a walk around the perimeter of the farm. He talked to them about types of hedging and rotation of crops. On the way back to the farm-yard, he stopped again, while he warned them of the dangers of pesticides. Several times he told the small group of boys, standing dangerously close to the ditch, to come away. It was the overflow from the slurry pit, on the other side of the hedge, he explained, and the sides were slippery. But, as usual, the warning fell on deaf ears. Ralph Raven seemed drawn towards it. He looked down with an evil grin on his face. The girls' gang didn't need to be mind-readers to know what he was thinking.

Sandra was still angry. The sight of Ralph standing there was too great a temptation. Jane could always tell what Sandra was thinking. It was one of the advantages of being a twin. Her first reaction was to stop Sandra. Common sense told her they'd never get away with it. But for once, common sense gave way to a natural desire for revenge. She smiled at Sandra. They nodded in agreement. They casually walked behind the group of boys and waited for their chance.

Stuart Harvey turned and saw them. He moved nervously aside, until he was directly behind Ralph. Sandra edged over. She quickly nudged him so that he tipped forward, propelling Ralph into the ditch. As Ralph slid the short distance down the bank, the girls, with one movement, grabbed Stuart by the jacket and pulled him back. Fortunately they were just in time to save him. Unfortunately they had to drag him through the thick, black mud in their brave attempt to rescue him.

"Look out!" Jane cried, as she clutched his collar.

"Don't worry, we've got you, Stuart," Sandra called out.

"We'll save you. You ought to be more careful," she said, as if talking to a naughty two-year-old. "Didn't you hear the farmer warning you to keep away?"

The sloppy liquid manure oozed over the top of Ralph's wellingtons and slowly poured in. He stood there, watching it happen. For a moment no one made a sound. Then Ralph broke into a wide, idiotic grin. The class hopped about with pleasure, until several of them looked in danger of joining him.

"Stand back, the rest of you," said Mr Mills, trying to keep a straight face. He would have liked to turn round and laugh his head off. But the prospect of Mr Thacker, the headmaster, waiting back at the school to greet them, wearing his superior expression, prevented Mr Mills from enjoying the joke. "Don't just stand there like an idiot paddling, Raven," he said. "Get out of there."

Ralph tried to lift his feet, one at a time.

"I can't, Sir," he said. "I seem to be stuck."

It took half an hour for the farmer and Mr Mills, standing on planks, to lever Ralph out of his wellingtons. The boots stood there, desolately peeping out above the slurry, like two abandoned boats. Ralph sat on the grass and peeled off his socks. He wiped the worst off, holding them well away from him.

"Pooh! He doesn't half pong," said Steven Sprigg, moving well away.

"We've never got to walk home with him, Sir, smelling like that!" said Melissa Whitehead, one of the fussier girls in the class.

"He doesn't smell any different to me," said Cheryl.

Back in the farmyard, the farmer hosed Ralph, from the knees down. Ralph enjoyed this and clowned around as if he were in a circus. Mr Mills shook his head. The farmer gave the class a short talk about the dangers of slurry pits. On this occasion it had seemed quite a joke but, he reminded them, it could have been far more serious. Nobody wanted to dwell on that thought.

Mr Mills thanked the farmer, who loaned Ralph a pair of boots to walk home in. With some prompting, Ralph and Stuart made their apologies.

Finally, Mr Mills said, "I think the least you two boys can do is to thank Sandra and Jane." Ralph and Stuart looked at the teacher open-mouthed. "Without their observation and quick thinking, both of you could have ended up in the ditch, in a much worse mess. You can have a house-point each, girls."

"Thank *them*?" said Ralph, nearly choking on the words.

"Yes, go on," said Mr Mills sternly. Ralph and Stuart mumbled something and curled their lips.

"Don't mention it," said Jane, smiling.

"I'm sure you'd have done the same thing, in our place," said Sandra sweetly.

"We certainly will," said Ralph, "if we ever get the chance."

Jo had watched it all out of the corner of her eye. She thought it was the neatest trick she'd seen. Perhaps there was more to these new girls than she had first thought. That Sandra clearly wasn't as daft as she looked. Ralph and Stuart, forced to walk home on the other side of the road, quietly plotted how they would get even with those girls if it was the last thing they did.

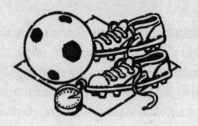

THE FOOTBALL
MATCH

The girls' gang were just about fed up with
Ralph Raven. He was the most big-headed boy
in the school. He thought he was so clever. He
was always interfering in what they were doing.
The girls' gang had been looking for another
chance to show everyone how stupid he was. But
when the opportunity came, Ralph didn't need
any help from them. He managed all on his
own.

One day in late November, Year 6 were sitting at
their tables listening to Mr Mills.

"This afternoon we are playing football against
North Street Junior School," he reminded them.
The boys didn't need reminding, most of them had
already changed into their football kit.

"Great!" cheered the boys. The girls remained silent.

"Fantastic!" said Ralph Raven. "Am I in goal, Sir?"

"I'm afraid you are," said Mr Mills.

"Aw, Sir! I'll be brilliant, honest. You watch. I'll move so fast nothing will get past me. I'll be like a human dynamo." Some of the girls began to giggle.

"That should be worth seeing," said Jane.

The girls' gang came and leaned on the teacher's desk while he began the daily search for the register. Mr Mills was not famous for his classroom organization. The surface of his desk looked like a children's party game: how many things can you balance on top of a table without anything falling off?

"What are the girls going to do this afternoon," asked Sandra, "since they won't be playing football?" Sandra was the dramatic twin. She made use of every opportunity to practise different roles. Today she was playing "the martyr".

"Well, you can come out and watch the match,' he said. The girls groaned.

"Or you can stay in and clean up the painting area."

"Cleaning up or football. What a choice," muttered Cheryl.

"How is it that girls always get the rotten jobs that nobody else wants to do?" said Jane.

"Natural selection?" suggested Stuart Harvey.

"You mean 'Survival of the thickest'," Cheryl replied. This was just one of Cheryl's own scientific theories.

"Oh, let's stay in," said Sandra.

"We could do a play," Louise suggested, "after we've finished clearing up."

"Better still, we could do a play before we do the clearing up," said Jane.

Mr Mills couldn't face another discussion with the twins about "girls' rights".

"Look, I don't mind which you do," he said, "as long as you don't disturb Miss Williams." Miss Williams was the teacher in the next classroom. She was extremely strict. All the children were scared of her. Even Mr Mills was scared of her and he didn't mind admitting it. To keep Miss Williams happy was one of his main aims in life.

"You make them do the cleaning up, Sir," said Ralph Raven. "They always get their own way, that lot."

"Footballers, get your boots on," said Mr Mills, ignoring Ralph. "The rest of you can collect your coats, then go out on to the field. And let's have no chanting today, it's a football match not a remedial choir practice."

As most of the class left the room, Mr Mills took a battered pair of plimsolls from the stock-cupboard. He carried them back to his desk. They were very old and grubby, with holes appearing where his toes had tried to escape. The girls leaned back a little as he put them on. Those plimsolls had supervised far more junior school football matches than Mr Mills would have liked to admit. In fact, given a whistle and a stop-watch, they could probably have done the job without him.

Ralph was sitting on the floor trying to tie his laces. The girls were watching him with obvious pleasure. The sight of Ralph Raven in difficulty always made them smile.

"Having trouble?" asked Sandra, in a sweet voice.

"Just get on with the cleaning up, you lot," he said.

With perfect timing, the five girls put their tongues out at him. They could do this almost without practice.

"Not a pretty sight," he said. "Let's hope you're good at cleaning up, nobody's going to marry any of you for your looks."

"We're not getting married," snapped Jo, "none of us." That was one of the girls' gang's resolutions: to have nothing to do with boys, especially don't marry one, ever!

"You'll change your minds," said Ralph, with a knowing smile. He got to his feet, ran his fingers through his hair and puffed out his chest. He stood for a moment, with his hands on his hips. Sandra did an excellent mime of someone being sick on the floor.

Meanwhile, Mr Mills was opening and closing drawers, with increasing impatience. Jo might have guessed this was not a good time to bother him, but she said:

"Sir, why can't I play for the team today? I'd be good in goal, better than him. You promised me a chance last time."

"Next time," said Mr Mills, searching for his stopwatch.

"You said if he let in any goals he was out of the team. He let in five!" Mr Mills was looking more and more harassed. Disturbing the debris on his desk again, he drew out a whistle on a long piece of grubby string. The pile quivered and began to slide. The girls leapt forward and caught things as they fell.

"Look, this is an important match," said Mr Mills. "If we win we go through to the next round. I can't put a girl in today. We need the best team we've got."

"Which is why I'm playing, eh, Sir?" said Ralph.

"We can't pick every one a winner, Ralph. This is absolutely your last chance. Let any through today and you're out."

"That's what you said last time," complained Jo.

The teacher pulled out the school football, from under his desk. He also found his stopwatch there.

"Come along, Ralph. Don't keep us waiting all day," said Mr Mills, and he jogged out on to the field. His hair, thinning on top, blew back in the wind, exposing a large amount of pink scalp. The girls watched this and smiled.

Jo leaned against Mr Mills' desk. She glared at Ralph Raven, as he pulled on his football shirt.

"You make me sick," she said. "If it wasn't for you I'd be in the team."

"Don't make me laugh," said Ralph. "He only lets you play at practices to humour you. Stick to cleaning up, I should. When you've finished, you can come out and watch me. We're going to walk all over them. Cry your heart out, North Street." Ralph waved his way out of the classroom.

"See you, fans," he said.

"What a pain," said Sandra. "I suppose his mother loves him."

"That's possible," said Jane. "Some people have no taste."

"It's not fair," said Jo. She kicked Ralph's clothes, from the heap where he had dropped them, into the far corner of the room. "I'm better than him. I'd like to show Ralph Raven. I'd like to show them all."

She went out of the door, teeth clenched and fists thrust into her pockets. The rest of the girls' gang watched her go. Louise's mum used to say Jo had a "bit of a chip on her shoulder". She was the youngest in the family of four brothers and she hated being the odd one out. Seeing her stamp across the field, Jane thought she looked as if she had a boulder, never mind a chip, on her shoulder.

The four girls had the classroom to themselves at last.

"Come on," said Sandra. "Let's do our play."

"But we ought to do the clearing up first," said Louise. Louise liked to do everything right. She was always worried about getting into trouble. The thought never occurred to Sandra.

"Oh, listen to Miss Too-good-to-be-true," she sneered.

"Let's get the cleaning up done first," said Cheryl, trying to keep the peace, "then we'll have lots of time for our play. I'll set my digital watch for five minutes. What isn't done then – too bad. On your marks . . . Get set . . . Go!"

The girls rushed round the room. Sandra collected scattered pieces of art paper and shuffled them into a neat pile. She rescued curled paintings from under desks and over radiators. All the while, she hummed and pretended to be Mary Poppins. Cheryl opened the art cupboard and gathered up everything which fell out at her feet. She found a set of maths books which had been missing a few weeks and a bag of hamster food. The hamster had died a fortnight ago; Cheryl hoped it hadn't been for lack of food. She found Ralph's P.E. bag, but she threw that to the back of the cuboard, and hid it under some tins of paint.

Jane and Louise washed the brushes and paint pots. Unfortunately, the water came out of the tap so fast they they were soon soaked. They spent a long time cleaning themselves up. Cheryl's watch began to bleep.

"OK, time girls," she called. They considered their handiwork for a moment. You could almost tell they'd done it, if you looked really hard.

"Let's do a play about Scheherazade," said Sandra. Her voice was heavy with drama and mystery. "I read about it in *Tales of the Arabian Nights*. It's about a king who doesn't like women. Every day he marries a new one, then has her head cut off. Soon there are hardly any young women left in the country."

"It's always the same with you, Sandra, nothing but sex and violence," said Cheryl.

"Eventually," Sandra continued, "he marries Scheherazade. She is very beautiful, but she's also clever. She manages to outwit him, by telling such wonderful stories that he can't bear to kill her."

"That'll be your part, I suppose," said Jane.

"Well, it was my idea," said Sandra. "Cheryl can be King. You can be my sister, who I tell the stories to."

"I don't want to be your sister. I get enough of that in real life. I have to listen to your stories all the rotten time,' Jane complained.

"OK, Louise can be my sister. You can be the palace guard. You can cut their heads off."

"Whose heads? There's no one left," Jane pointed out.

"We'll get Jo in later," said Sandra. "She can have her head cut off."

"She'll love that," said Cheryl. "Still, I suppose it will take her mind off football."

The girls' gang often made up plays. It was their favourite pastime. Their plays usually followed the same pattern. The longest job was deciding who should play each character. This always involved arguments about who had the best part. At some point one or two of them would swop. Later there would be more disagreement about who had played the part best. Then they might swop back. Sometimes they'd forget they'd swopped back and find themselves playing two parts at the same time. It could be very confusing.

Today's play was like this, but, in addition, they found themselves short of actresses. Louise was sent to find Jo to try to persuade her to come in and have her head chopped off. She met Jo as she was walking off the field.

"Has it finished?" Louise asked.

"Not quite, but I can't bear to watch any more."

Ralph Raven had let in two goals. The score was 2-2 and they were about to play ten minutes' extra time. When he let in the second goal, Jo had gone mad. She had called Ralph such a rude name that Mr Mills had "sent her off".

"I told him I wasn't even playing," she said, "but he gave me a nasty look and the finger."

Back in the classroom she grumbled to the other girls.

"Well, it's a good job," said Sandra. "Because we need you in our play now. You're a young girl who is going to have her head cut off. You have to cry and beat your breast and beg to be set free. Like this." Sandra fell to her knees. She beat herself with her fists and tore wildly at her hair. All the while she sobbed hysterically and implored the others to set her free.

The girls watched in amazement. They never ceased to be impressed by Sandra's acting. They often found it embarrassing, but, at the same time, it was exciting. You never could be sure what she might do next. Jo was not as easily impressed. She still thought Sandra was a bit of a show-off. And today she had other things on her mind.

"You'll have to wait," she said. "I want to see the last few minutes through the window."

Sandra picked herself up from the floor and dusted her knees.

"Please yourself. We'll have to try and manage without you," she said.

So the girls continued with their play, each one interfering with what the others had to say.

"Look, this is my part, I'm the King," complained Cheryl. "You say your own lines, or I'll have your head chopped off."

"But I'm the executioner," said Jane.

Jo was sitting on top of a desk with her back to the girls, watching the match. A few metres from the window, Ralph Raven was standing in goal.

"Just come and look at this," said Jo. "The

Human Dynamo!" The girls joined her. They soon picked out the familiar figure.

Ralph was leaning heavily against the goal-post. All the action was at the other end of the pitch, and had been for some time. Ralph looked bored. He'd been out there an hour, with hardly anything to do. The ball had only come his way twice in the whole game. He started to shiver, so he decided to jog on the spot. This made him feel better. He did some limbering-up exercises, a few arm swings, a couple of press-ups, half a dozen knee bends.

That was more like it. He ran up and down the goal mouth a couple of times. Next he started his own private game. He began to save imaginary goals. There were some really tough ones. They took all his immense skill and dazzling speed to control.

First, he leapt up into the right-hand corner, arms outstretched. He made a miraculous save with the very tips of his fingers, clawing it back through the air. He threw the ball to his team, waving away their congratulations. Then he fell headlong in the mud, across the mouth of the goal. It was like dropping a drawbridge. The goal was impregnable. He hugged the ball to him, before throwing it back to his admiring team-mates.

Next, he blocked an otherwise certain goal by

throwing himself at the feet of another player and grinding the ball into the ground. The imaginary cheers were deafening. He ran out to meet the other players, to receive their hugs and kisses. He jogged back and forwards, arms raised in triumph, nodding and waving to the crowd. He even seemed to be trying to pat himself on the back.

The girls' gang watched the whole performance.

"We could do with him in our plays," said Jane. The girls couldn't stop laughing. It was making Sandra's stomach ache. They banged on the window and clapped and cheered. Ralph turned and saw them. He grinned, then took a few bows. Ralph Raven couldn't resist an audience. The girls cheered louder and banged on the window for more.

Ralph was happy to oblige. He started to jump up and down and beat his chest like Tarzan. Then he ran around the goal area, with his arms hanging low down around his ankles, his fists swinging loosely in front of him. The girls could almost hear him making monkey noises.

"Ugh-ugh-ugh-ugh," said Ralph Raven.

By now, the girls were making a lot of noise. Miss Williams sent some children from her class to find out what was going on. But the girls were laughing so much they couldn't even answer. Ralph made a few leaps and managed to catch hold of the cross-bar. He began to swing hand over hand, from one end to the other. He was still making monkey noises and he stopped, from time to time, to scratch his head, or under his arms. He picked off an imaginary flea and ate it.

Ralph could see the girls' faces. He was really enjoying himself. But then, he noticed that the children in the next room were crowding by their window and watching him too. He could see Miss Williams' disapproving face. They were all watching him hanging there, pretending to be an orangutan. But the girls weren't clapping and cheering now. They were waving their arms wildly and then pointing, as if they were trying to tell him something.

He could see Jo's mouth opening and closing like a goldfish. But he couldn't hear anything, not through the window. He strained forward, just in case. He might have been able to hear, after all they weren't far away, if it hadn't suddenly got so noisy. A real row had started up, right behind him. It was nearly deafening. You'd have thought Mr Mills would have put a stop to that kind of noise.

Still clutching the cross-bar, Ralph turned his head to see what it was all about. Something white and round and rather familiar, flew at speed, under his dangling legs, and smacked against the net. It dropped to the floor and rolled beneath him. It took only a couple of seconds for the truth to sink in.

They'd scored! Those lousy, rotten devils had sneaked up, the moment his back was turned, and scored a goal. The deciding goal as well. It wasn't fair! You'd have thought somebody could have warned him. And there was the final whistle. Now they'd lost and he would get the blame. Those flaming girls, he'd fix them, if it was the last thing he did.

In the classroom the girls' gang could see Ralph, still hanging from the cross-bar. His face was a strange colour and his eyes looked in danger of popping out of his head. His mouth was working furiously. You didn't have to be able to lip-read to make out what he was saying. It was a good job he had his back to Mr Mills. He'd have sent him off for certain.

Ralph hadn't thought to get down yet. He was too stunned to move. But a large hand had grabbed him from behind and, with a sharp pull, was trying to get him down.

"It's all right, Ralph, you can let go now," said Mr Mills, between gritted teeth. "You needn't be afraid. We won't let that nasty, big ball get you, will we, lads?"

Ralph was worried, as he walked into the classroom. There was the kind of atmosphere he recognized from old cowboy films, where somebody is about to get lynched. And he had a good idea who that might be.

"I only took my eyes off it for a second, Sir, honest. It wasn't my fault. It was those stupid girls. They kept banging on the window and distracting me. You ought to tell them off, Sir. They were supposed to be cleaning up. Just look at this place. I could do better myself. The only thing they're good at is causing trouble."

"I wish I could find something *you're* good at, Raven," said Mr Mills.

"He's pretty good at acting, Sir," said Jane. "We could put him in one of our plays."

"There aren't many plays with orang-utans in," said Cheryl. "Can you think of any, Sandra?"

You could tell Sandra was having one of her ideas. She had that faraway look in her eyes. It was going to be another epic performance.

"What about *King Kong*?" she said.

For a moment, Ralph looked quite interested.

THE CHRISTMAS
PARTY

It was nearly the last week of term and the girls
were getting excited. Everyone in the class felt the
same, now that it was so close to Christmas. Lots
of good things happened in school at this time of
year. The best thing of all was the Christmas Party.
But this year the class almost missed their party
because all the party money disappeared. Mr Mills
said that was the final straw.

At Witton Park Primary School, the Year 6 party
was different from other Years. It was held after
school, when everyone else had gone home. Year 6
pupils had to come back in the dark, wearing their
best clothes. Instead of bringing a jelly or a packet
of crisps, like the younger children, they brought
money. Mr Mills took his car down to the local

chip shop and bought them fish and chips, or sausage and chips, and ice-cream for afters.

"Shouldn't we be collecting for the party, Sir?" asked Sandra, one morning, while Mr Mills was marking her maths book.

"Oh, plenty of time for that," said Mr Mills. "You concentrate on your work. There'll be distractions soon enough."

There was the familiar, painful sound of several children tuning violins outside, in the open-area. Most of the class instinctively pressed their fingers in their ears.

"Roll on Boxing Day," he muttered.

"Sir, you sound like Scrooge this morning,' said Sandra.

"This morning, I feel like Scrooge," he said.

It had been a long, difficult term. There had been early snow, measles and trouble with the school boiler. By now everyone was tired, particularly Mr Mills. And there was still worse to come. He had spent the last two evenings, after school, climbing up and down step-ladders, arranging the lights for the Christmas Carol Concert. This was Mr Thacker's favourite event in the school calendar. Preparing for it, the whole school seemed to come to a standstill. Mr Thacker had worked the choir so hard that some of the younger children were now away from school with nervous exhaustion. Mr Mills sympathized with them. He felt worn out himself. He would like to have been one of those infants, wrapped up in bed with a hot-water bottle, right now.

The lighting for the concert was Mr Mills' responsibility. Every year he dreaded it. The lights were old and heavy. It took him hours to get them hung, only to find that half of them were no longer working. And there was another problem, which he wouldn't have confessed to anyone: he was terrified of heights. Just standing on a chair could make him dizzy. He'd always had this vague fear of falling and breaking something. Last night it had happened. He had made the mistake of allowing Ralph Raven, and Stuart Harvey to hold the bottom of the steps. Of course, he had fallen off and badly sprained his ankle.

Mr Mills winced with pain as he lifted his bandaged leg on to a low stool. This morning he felt he had every reason to sulk. He wasn't in the least bit interested in Christmas celebrations.

Cheryl brought out her book to be marked.

"Sir, _we_ could arrange the party, if you don't feel up to it." Mr Mills hesitated, which was a mistake. Sensing the weakness across the room, the girls surrounded him.

"You leave it to the girls' gang, Sir," said Sandra, saluting and standing to attention.

"Yeah, we'll do it," said Jane.

"We'll organize everything," said Jo.

"You needn't give it another thought," said Louise, patting his arm. Mr Mills' heart sank. Why couldn't anyone protect him from these girls?

He had always enjoyed taking Year 6. He had taught that age for nearly ten years now. He liked the way you knew where you were with them. By this stage, they'd been pretty well moulded into shape. But this group of girls was different. It wasn't that they were badly behaved or refused to get their work done; it was the fact that they wouldn't keep quiet and leave him alone. They were so persistent. They were forever coming up with some new scheme to disrupt the class. And they wouldn't just do the jobs they were given. They always had to have a half-hour discussion about whether it was fair or not. Fair! Whoever pretended that schools were fair?

But today Mr Mills had no energy to resist them.

"All right, Cheryl. Collect the money in by Friday. We'll talk about the games next week."

People brought their money each day and Cheryl collected it. She put it in an old tobacco tin, marked "BLU-TACK". Mr Mills' drawer was full of these carefully labelled tins from the happy days when he had smoked a pipe. Recently his children had made him give it up. They told him it was a disgusting habit. Now he only had the tins, as reminders. Sometimes, when he took the lid off one, to get a rubber band, he would catch the smell. His whole face would light up with pleasure. Watching this from her table, Cheryl nudged Jane and whispered:

"Look at him. Talk about glue-sniffing."

By Friday afternoon everyone had brought in their money, except Ralph Raven. The girls made a ring around his table and tried to look threatening.

"Where's your money?" asked Cheryl. Ralph ignored her. He was drawing a detailed picture of a battle. There were several hundred pin-sized soldiers, all firing guns at one another. Judging by the amount of red felt pen he had used, nearly everyone had been hit.

"Trust you to be the only one who hasn't paid yet," said Sandra, bringing her hand down heavily on his table.

"Oh, help, save me. It's the Mafia," said Ralph, putting up his hands in surrender.

"If you don't bring it on Monday, you won't be allowed to go to the party," said Jo.

"Oh no? And who's going to stop me?" Ralph sneered at the girls. "The Famous Five?"

"Well, you'll be the only one who doesn't get any fish and chips," said Louise.

"Perhaps your pal, Stuart Harvey, will save you a chip or two," said Jane.

The idea of Stuart Harvey giving anybody anything to eat was so ridiculous, even Ralph had to smile. Stuart Harvey had brought enough money for two portions of chips, a fish and a sausage. And everyone knew he would still try to pinch other people's food.

At home-time, Cheryl counted out the money. There was over twenty pounds. She put it back in the tin and gave it to Mr Mills for safe-keeping. He put it into his pocket. He was getting ready to go to the Hall for the dress rehearsal of the Carol Concert. He was searching his desk, which was hidden beneath a mountain of unfinished Christmas decorations. He was looking for another tin, which might contain a packet of fuses. He was bound to need them before the rehearsal was over. He found two tins marked "FUSES"; one was empty, the other full of magnets. The tins piled up and fell noisily to the floor, setting his teeth on edge. At the best of times he was untidy, but, under pressure, Mr Mills drifted helplessly towards chaos.

His days had been disrupted by a trail of interruptions. Baby angels and infant shepherds had wandered in and out, asking for the impossible.

"Please, Sir. Have you got some Blu-Tack?"

"Miss Williams says, 'Have you any spare selotape?'"

"Can we borrow some sharp scissors to trim my wings with?"

These things were always in short supply and by this stage in the term they were like gold. If he'd had any, Mr Mills would have hidden them, rather than let them out of his sight. Christmas preparations in school seemed to bring out the worst in everyone.

It was mainly Mr Thacker's fault. He was running this concert as if it were a military operation. At intervals throughout the day he sent runners with messages.

"Mary and Joseph and members of the choir – report to the Hall." "Send six large boys to move furniture."

And, of course, that started those wretched girls off again. They insisted they could do anything the

66

boys could do. They moaned that it wasn't fair to choose Ralph Raven every time, just because he was the strong and stupid type.

"Strong and silent, you mean," said Stuart Harvey.

"Not in his case," said Jane.

And now Mr Mills was getting more irritated. The class had been told they could go, but no one seemed in a hurry. There were children hanging around his desk, as though they had no homes to go to. He sent Louise off with a few sharp words. She had moved a pile of choir sheets, scattering paper chains in all directions. Finally, he found a tin marked "RUBBER BANDS", which rattled. It contained the missing fuses. As he started to push the other tins back into the drawer a five-year-old, wearing a Dangermouse dressing gown and a tea-towel over his head, appeared by Mr Mills' desk.

"Please, Sir," he said. "Mr Thacker says, 'Is Mr Mills coming today, or should the rest of us pack up and go home?'"

Mr Mills said something quietly under his breath. The five-year-old blushed under his tea-towel.

By the time Mr Mills reached the Hall, the noise was deafening. Mr Thacker was having a quick cup of tea, with the ancillary, in the staff-room. Taking advantage of this, a number of children had started fighting. Two angels were sitting on a wise man and trying to tickle him to death, while the inn-keeper twisted Mary's arm behind her back, until the tears came. Joseph stood by grinning. The shepherds were sliding, in their stockinged feet, across the polished wood floor, using the back of the piano to stop themselves. One boy, who had missed and collided with the wall-bars, was sitting holding his head and howling. No one took any notice. One little vandal was relieving his boredom by drawing a felt-pen moustache on the baby Jesus, as he lay asleep in the crib. Mr Mills put the fuse tin safely on the radiator shelf. He hid it, among the decorations, away from prying fingers. Watching the acts of violence around him, he muttered to himself, "Season of goodwill, a likely story!"

At five o'clock, Mr Mills returned to the class-room. He had the kind of headache, described by those cartoon pictures, where someone is walking around with an axe buried in his head. He couldn't face tidying up now. He quickly swept a hand across the surface of the desk, scooping the pile of tins into the drawer. It was at this point that he remembered the tin of party money, which Cheryl had given him. He checked his pockets. Only a tin of fuses. Then he took each of the dozens of tins, rattled them and checked them yet again. By 5.15 he had to accept that the money was gone. It must have been stolen. If so, then it must have been taken by someone from Year 6. Well, he'd had enough of children this term. That was absolutely the final straw. He went home and brooded about it all weekend.

On Monday morning, Year 6 sat at their tables. They were looking at Mr Mills, but nobody wanted to catch his eye. Everyone felt uncomfortable and embarrassed. They hadn't stolen the money, but someone in the room had. Mr Mills said, unless the person owned up by 3.30 there would be no party and no fish and chips.

During break the girls sat miserably on the climbing frame. They were doubly disappointed. They had organized the party games and even prepared one of their famous plays. They were trying to work out who it might have been, in the hope that they could be made to own up.

"Now, we need to be scientific about this," said Cheryl.

"There are thirty-two people in our class, that leaves twenty-seven suspects."

"What about the other five?" said Louise.

"That's us, dopey. We didn't do it, did we?"

"I think we should all swear we didn't do it, just in case," said Sandra, dramatically spitting on her fingers.

"I swear I didn't do it," said the four girls in turn.

"I didn't do it," said Louise, making the Girl Guide salute. "I'm not allowed to swear, or spit."

"OK, let's try to eliminate a few more," said Cheryl.

They ticked off those in the nativity, the choir, the bus children and a number of others considered too timid to be suspected. They also crossed off Michael Flynn and Anthony Kariolis, the class chess fiends. The only thing they'd ever be likely to steal was a chess set and they already owned ten sets between them. The gang were left with two girls and half a dozen boys. There was the inevitable name of Ralph Raven.

"Need we look any further?" said Sandra.

"We must have proof," said Cheryl. "You can't convict anyone without evidence, even Ralph Raven."

"Sometimes," said Sandra, "you don't need proof. You just have a feeling."

But Cheryl insisted that Mr Mills would want proof. And it was up to them to get it.

At dinner-time the girls stayed inside, putting up the last of the snow-flake decorations on the classroom window.

"Aren't they lovely?" said Louise. She stood back to admire them.

"They're all right, but they'll only be up a couple of days and it will be time to take them down," grumbled Jo.

Cheryl was going through Ralph Raven's drawer, while Sandra searched his P.E. bag. Jane was standing guard outside in the open area.

"Pity we can't check his jacket," said Cheryl.

"He never takes the rotten thing off," said Jo.

Ralph had a denim jacket which he wore every day. It was a kind of trademark; you never saw him without it.

"I bet he sleeps in it," said Sandra.

She put her hand over her nose. "And I hate to think how long it is since this P.E. kit was washed," she said.

"Look at this!" said Cheryl. She held out an exercise book of Ralph's. It was full of cartoons.

Ralph Raven spent a lot of time drawing. It was

one thing he was good at, particularly cartoons. Opening the book and flipping through the pages, Cheryl had immediately picked out a number of familiar faces: Mr Mills, other teachers and some people from Year 6. There was a large group of five extremely stupid-looking monkeys, wearing Wonder Woman outfits. Across their chests were the letters "G.G." The five girls were all recognizable, even though each of them was actually a monkey. The one that was Sandra was holding a mirror up to her face and, with big lips, was kissing her own reflection. Underneath it said, "The Gibbon Gang". The girls were mad.

From now on, war on Ralph Raven was officially declared. The girls' gang were determined to prove he had stolen the money. But as Cheryl pointed out, he could already have spent it. If so, how could they ever find out?

"We can ask his sister," suggested Louise. "She's in the same class as our Alice."

"Oh, yeah," said Jo. "That's a great idea. Then she'd go straight back and tell him."

"Not if we ask in a roundabout way, drop it casually in the conversation," said Sandra, private investigator. "You've got to be subtle. Leave it to me."

They found Ralph's sister, Stephanie, propped

up against her friend Debra. They were sharing a Mars bar. The plump five-year-olds looked like a pair of book-ends. The girls' gang stood nearby, secretly watching them. The two little girls openly watched them back. Sandra struggled to think of an innocent question, but couldn't. The others waited hopefully. They could see the dinner-ladies, about to blow the whistle for afternoon school. At last, she blurted out,

"What does your Ralph do at weekends?"

Stephanie stared at her.

"I mean, what did he do this weekend, anything special?"

"He took me shopping, to buy my mam's present.'

"Oh, did he," interrupted Sandra, "and did *he* buy anything?" The girls moved in closer.

"No, he's too mean. Our Ralph never buys for anybody else."

"Are you sure he didn't buy anything, all weekend?" Sandra pressed her.

"No, nothing, he's broke. He's got to pay for next door's window. He smashed it in the summer. He said he was practising golf but my dad said, 'A likely story!'"

The whistle blew. The girls' gang wandered away, disappointment on their faces.

"What d'you suppose they really wanted?" said Debra, taking her thumb out of her mouth and drying it on her skirt.

"They fancy our Ralph, of course, specially that fair-haired one. I'll tell him, when I get home. It's time he had a girl-friend, my mam says. Perhaps he'd start cleaning his teeth then."

After school the girls' gang decided to follow Ralph home. He must still have the money. He might be planning to spend it on the way. They kept well behind, but never let him out of their sight. When he stopped at the newsagent's shop at the end of the road, Jo followed him in. As the girls waited, their hopes rose.

"I thought she said he had no money," said Sandra.

"Caught red-handed," said Jane.

"Let's wait and see," said Cheryl.

But when Jo came out she had discovered nothing. Ralph had been buying a comic and a magazine. He'd looked embarrassed when Jo walked in. She thought she had caught him out this time. But he had said to her:

"The *Beano*'s for me and the *Woman's Own*'s for my mam, before you make any cracks." Then he'd rolled them both up and hit her on the head with them, as he went out.

"Not what you'd call big spending," said Cheryl.

The girls hung around, near his house, hoping something would happen. It started to rain. The girls huddled together against a hedge. They were cold and wet. Inside the house Stephanie was watching them, from behind the living-room curtains.

"Ralph, them girls are still outside; the ones who fancy you. They must be keen, standing about in the rain," she said. "That's the one, the fair-haired twin. She's mad on you. Are you going to ask her out?"

Ralph was engrossed in a cartoon on T.V. He never moved his eyes. "Yeah, I might," he said. After half an hour the girls gave up and went home.

The next day at school the girls observed Ralph for any signs of nervousness or guilt, but Ralph was his usual loud self; if anything, more so. From time to time Sandra turned round to find Ralph watching her. Once or twice she thought he had winked at her. The idea was horrific. She told herself she must have imagined it. The day dragged slowly on. There was no sign of Mr Mills changing his mind. There was now little chance of anyone owning up before home-time. The party had been planned for the next day. This afternoon was the last opportunity to rearrange it. Everyone in the class felt cheated and bad-tempered. People were bickering about nothing in particular.

Sandra could see the clock on the blackboard wall. The end of the day was coming closer. By three o'clock she couldn't sit still on her chair. Her face was flushed and she was grinding her teeth. Jane recognized the sound. It was usually a bad sign. Sandra stood up and took a deep breath.

"You'll just get us all into trouble," said Jane, pulling Sandra's sweater, to make her sit down.

"Oh, Sandra, don't," said Louise.

"You can't do it," said Cheryl. "You've no proof."

"I don't care," said Sandra. She walked over to the teacher's desk.

"Mr Mills . . . Sir."

Mr Mills looked up with a weary face. "What is it?"

"It's about the stolen money . . ." said Sandra.

"What about it?" The class was silent. Thirty-one pairs of eyes turned and focused themselves on Sandra's back.

"I think I know . . ."

At that moment, Mr Thacker came into the classroom. He seemed pleased with himself. He wore that sticky, self-satisfied look your mother wears when she has proved herself right and you wrong yet again. In his hand he was carrying one of Mr Mills' tobacco tins.

"Yours, I think," he said.

"Thank you," said Mr Mills, hardly glancing at the tin. His attention was still on Sandra.

"I found it in the Hall, on the shelf," said Mr Thacker.

"Yes, thank you! It's my fuses."

"Says 'BLU-TACK'," said Mr Thacker, evidently enjoying himself.

"Yes, but it contains fuses," said Mr Mills sharply.

Mr Thacker rattled the tin close to Mr Mills' ear.

"Doesn't sound like fuses, does it?" he said.

By the expression on Mr Mills' face Sandra knew in a second. It took the rest of the class minutes to work it out. Slowly it dawned on each of them, as if little lights were going on all over the room. One by one they began to smile. Mr Thacker was the sort of person who seemed to enjoy other people's discomfort. He was loving it.

While she had the chance, Sandra crept back to her table. Mr Thacker left the room, whistling. Embarrassed silence rose up and hung in the air, so that you could almost hear it. Everyone struggled not to smile. One or two people, who couldn't help it, covered their mouths with their hands. After what felt like a long time, Mr Mills said:

"Don't forget to bring your party clothes with you, bus children. Cheryl, I'll see the list of games in the morning. You can go home." And without another word, that is just what they all did.

The next day the class tiptoed around Mr Mills, as though he was wired and might go off at any moment. He was in a terrible mood. Cheryl showed him the list of games. He nodded his approval. During the afternoon he sent the girls' gang into the Hall to arrange the tables and chairs. They were relieved to get out of the classroom, to be able to breathe freely without upsetting the teacher.

"I hope Mr Mills cheers up a bit before 4.30, or it's going to be a miserable party," complained Sandra.

"At least we've got a party," said Jo.

"I feel sick every time I think how close you came to telling Mr Mills it was Ralph Raven," said Jane.

"I did try to tell you we needed some proof," said Cheryl, "but, oh no . . ."

"OK, OK. You were right," admitted Sandra. "Don't go on about it. I still say it *could* have been him."

"Oh, Sandra," said the others.

"For once, can't you admit when you're in the wrong?" snapped Jane. Sandra went very quiet.

The party was a success. After the first few minutes even Mr Mills began to relax and enjoy himself, despite his bad ankle. Miss Williams offered to collect the fish and chips. This unexpected kindness made Mr Mills feel less and less like Scrooge. The girls' gang performed a short play about Hallowe'en. Stuart Harvey said it was not exactly seasonal. But everyone clapped hard and laughed a lot, especially when Jo's mask kept slipping. This disgusted Sandra. She hated people to laugh in the wrong places.

Then they played musical statues, "Marks and Spencer's" and other team games. Melissa Whitehead sulked when her team lost, but everyone ignored her.

At the end of the party, Mr Mills asked them to gather round. They waited for him to speak, but he kept on staring at the ceiling. He seemed to have forgotten what he was going to say. Eventually he looked directly at them. His eyes were full up.

"I'd like to say I'm sorry," he said.

It took a little while for some of the class to realize what he was talking about. They shuffled uncomfortably. No one could lift their eyes from the floor. This was far worse than being told off, or accused of something they hadn't done. Those things happened every day, but they didn't know how to deal with this. Some people struggled not to giggle. They knew it was not a giggling matter. It felt as if they might be there for hours, waiting for someone to break the silence. Then Sandra stepped forward. Jane watched her in horror. Whatever was she going to say now?

"I think I should say sorry, as well, Sir."

"What for, Sandra?"

"Because I thought it was Ralph that had done it."

"Thanks very much," said Ralph. Several of the class laughed, too loudly.

"We've been following him round, trying to find proof. I know we were wrong and I'm sorry."

"That's all right," said Ralph generously. Sandra stepped back and the rest of the gang smiled at her.

"Actually," said Ralph. "I did think, at first, that your little gang might have done it." Sandra nearly exploded at this. "But when you kept on following me about, I decided it was most likely 'cos you fancied me."

"Aghghghgh!" screamed Sandra, struggling to get at him. The other girls wisely held her back.

"Anyway, I'll forgive you, since it's supposed to be the season of goodwill. After all, you're only girls." And Ralph smiled at Sandra and gave her a big wink.

Mr Mills looked at the girls' faces. Perhaps over the holidays they might forget, but somehow he doubted it. He has a feeling they wouldn't let Ralph Raven get away with that. And, of course, he was quite right.

THE SCHOOL TRIP

Every year, at the end of February, Mr Mills took his class away on a school trip, to a hostel called "Fernlea". It was on the edge of a village. They stayed there from Monday to Friday, doing environmental studies and going out on visits. The class thought it was brilliant. Mr Mills didn't always share that opinion. It could be very hard work. Many of them had never stayed away from home before and sometimes they got over-excited. They did silly things, like trapping their fingers in doors, or falling out of top bunks and breaking arms or legs. The week hardly seemed complete without a trip to the local hospital. But this year Mr Mills was determined to bring them all back without even minor injuries. Unfortunately, this aim didn't take account of the girls' gang and their long-running battle with Ralph Raven, not to mention "Claude the Ghost".

MONDAY

Cheryl's "Fernlea" Diary

> It will be very interesting this week, to see how certain species adapt to a new environment and habitat. Louise looks like a fish out of water away from her mum. Will she survive?

The bus turned into the village.

"We're nearly there," said Mr Mills. "Try not to leave anything on the coach." At intervals on the two-hour journey Louise had been remembering a list of things she had already left at home. She couldn't stop talking. She was feeling nervous. This would be the first time she had ever slept out of her own bed.

"Are you all right?" said Jane. "You do look a funny colour."

"I think I feel sick" said Louise. Jo quickly moved further along the seat.

Miss Williams, who was accompanying them on the trip, picked up the dreaded word. She had a phobia about it. The main thing she disliked about children was that they seemed to be so easily sick. She considered it a lack of self-discipline. At times she suspected they did it just to spite her. Miss Williams turned and gave Louise one of her early warning signals. Louise looked quickly out of the window and swallowed hard. She wasn't sure that she was going to enjoy this week.

On their arrival, Year 6 stood outside the bus. They waited, in the fine February drizzle, as their cases were unloaded. Across the road, the girls considered the large, bleak building in which they would be staying. Once, when the village was much bigger, it had been a school. Now it was a hostel, covered with a thick growth of ivy. The windows, which were divided into small leaded lights, made the place appear even gloomier. Opposite the hostel stood the village church and in front of it was a sinister-looking graveyard.

"I don't like this place," said Louise.

"Oh, don't be mardy," said Jo.

"But it looks as if it might be haunted."

Overhearing their conversation, Ralph Raven put his jacket over his head. Approaching Louise from behind, he moaned, "Whoooooooooooooooooooooooooo!"

To everyone's surprise, Louise burst into tears.

"I want to go home," she said.

"Now see what you've done, you great baboon," said Jo. She pushed Ralph roughly aside. Still hidden under his jacket, he staggered backwards into the row of waiting suitcases. They fell, like skittles, in all directions. One large case, grossly over-full, burst open, spilling its contents into the gutter. These included a few clothes and what seemed to be the entire contents of a cake-shop. The suitcase belonged to Stuart Harvey. He had been worried that he might not get enough to eat on this trip.

Mr Mills came round the corner of the bus. Ralph Raven lay spread-eagled among the suitcases; Stuart Harvey was scrabbling in the road to retrieve packets of doughnuts and Jaffa Cakes; Louise was being comforted by the other girls. Several mouths began to open in explanation.

"Don't tell me," said Mr Mills. "I'd rather not know."

At the doorway to the hostel stood a short, seedy-looking man. He had a sharp nose, bushy eyebrows and small, sunken eyes. He resembled a crafty animal. He wore working clothes and a check, flat cap. His name was Mr Sutton.

"Wipe your feet and mind your manners," he greeted everyone. Despite his rough appearance, they recognized him as a person of considerable authority. He was clearly the caretaker. He eyed Louise's tear-stained face and added:

"Don't you go dribbling on my clean floors." His face twitched, after this last remark, which was the only indication that he had made a joke.

Inside the building the February gloom persisted. The long corridors were unlit. People bumped into one another, shrieking as they struggled with suitcases, bags of wellingtons and damp coats. On reaching their dormitory, the girls heaped their things in the middle of the floor. Their room was plain and roughly decorated. There were two pairs of bunks, a single bed, two wardrobes, a chest of drawers and a pink wicker chair. At the end of the single bed was a white plastic bucket. It was collecting the drips of rain which had found their way through the leaky roof. The constant plop! plop! plop! was like a sixth person trying to hog the conversation.

Louise sat on the single bed, undecided whether to stay. She was feeling homesick. While the others unpacked, she sucked her thumb and wound a long piece of hair round and round her finger.

"Come on, Louise, you and me'll share a bunk," said Jane.

"What about me?" said Sandra. She had discovered a full-length mirror on the back of the door.

She was busy practising faces in front of it. While she talked, or unpacked her case, Sandra watched herself. Her eyes were drawn like magnets to the mirror. The other girls pretended not to notice.

"We'll have this bunk, Jo," said Cheryl. "You can go on top."

Still in her coat and shoes, Jo swung herself up. The bunks, old and rickety, lurched from side to side. Cheryl could see how you might get sea-sick, sleeping in the same bunk as Jo.

"Don't anybody worry about me," said Sandra, banging her case down on the single bed. "I suppose someone has to be the odd-one-out . . . pushed off on their own . . . ignored . . . neglected . . ." Sandra was so carried away by her own performance, which she was watching in the mirror, that she didn't notice the other girls smiling. They picked up their pillows and crept up on her from behind.

Mr Mills, always on the look-out for any early signs of trouble, put his head round the door. "Don't murder her in the dormitory," he advised them. "Mr Sutton wouldn't appreciate the mess."

The first afternoon was always spent on a long walk, to the top of a nearby hill, known locally as "Barney's Mount". It was a regular part of Mr Mills' strategy to try and tire them out and help some people to work up an appetite. Stuart Harvey didn't need any help. At supper-time, he ate five bowls of soup, with half a loaf of bread, and three helpings of shepherd's pie. Then he went back to his room, for a packet of iced buns to finish off with.

Cheryl watched him eat with the same rapt attention with which David Attenborough might study a deadly snake. She scribbled observations in her science notebook.

"It's remarkable really," she said. "He doesn't even stop to chew. He just seems to swallow it whole. Like those snakes that can eat a small buffalo by stretching their throats. I think it's fascinating."

"I think it's disgusting," said Jane. "He's nothing but a human vacuum cleaner."

"Can you imagine what his stomach looks like?" said Sandra.

Jo made a noise that resembled a sink emptying. Louise clutched her hand to her mouth and rushed to the toilets.

At breakfast-time on Tuesday there were a number of tired faces. In the excitement of their first night away from home, most people had done very little sleeping. Mr Mills had spent hours patrolling the corridors, sending them back to bed. Consequently, this morning, they were all much quieter. Miss Williams was the only person who still looked sharp and alert. Mr Mills was even having trouble finding his mouth with the spoon.

The girls' gang were keeping Louise company, while she stirred a few cornflakes round her bowl.

"Now, come on, eat it up. Don't play with it," said Mr Sutton, the caretaker. "You'd have been better with porridge. Puts hairs on your chest does porridge."

Sandra pulled a face. She'd already seen the porridge. It looked like quick-set cement. It was Cheryl's opinion that Mr Sutton probably did the cooking, as well as caretaking. He certainly took a personal interest in how much you ate. The girls didn't like the way he hovered around the place. Even for a caretaker he was extraordinarily bossy.

When Ralph Raven and Stuart Harvey sidled up to their table, the girls' gang groaned. It wasn't enough to put them off. The boys sat down.

"If you're not going to eat that toast, I'll have it,' said Stuart Harvey.

"Watch out, here come the vultures," said Jane.

Louise pushed it towards him. The girls watched in dreadful fascination. He spread both pieces thickly with jam, sandwiched them together and then ate the lot in three large bites.

"You deserve to be sick," said Jo.

"Not me," said Stuart, wiping the excess jam on

the leg of his jeans. "Never been sick in my life."

"Well, if you are, make sure it's not on my floors," said Mr Sutton, eavesdropping again. They were the only people left in the dining-room. As they got up to go, Mr Sutton lowered his voice and said,

"Have any of you met Claude, yet?"

"Who's Claude?" asked Sandra.

"Claude's the ghost," said Mr Sutton.

The faces around the table displayed a range of feelings: sheer panic on Louise's, disbelief on Cheryl's and evil pleasure on Ralph's.

"Who was this Claude?" asked Ralph, grinning.

"Used to be headmaster here, when it was a school. He was really barmy, so they say."

"Barmy?" asked Cheryl.

"You know, a bit strange." He tapped the side of his head with a rough, blackened finger-nail. He lowered his voice further and added:

"Most teachers are, haven't you noticed?"

"Yes, and most caretakers too," thought Cheryl.

Mr Sutton went on, "He did weird things, like hiding in the boiler-room, doing crosswords, every morning."

This didn't impress them much. They thought all headmasters spent their time as they pleased. Mr Thacker certainly did.

"And he had an obsession with keys," said Mr Sutton. "He was forever locking up, even in the middle of the day. He'd go round, locking classroom doors, with classes still inside."

"So what happened to him in the end?" said Ralph, wanting to get to the nasty part.

"Well, he had a bit of a brainstorm. First he set light to the bicycle sheds, then he climbed to the top of the church tower and fell off. They say he was drunk. Dead drunk." And his face twitched. This was obviously the part of the story he liked.

Ralph Raven was enjoying it too.

"He must have landed S P L A T!" he said, bringing his hand down heavily on the table, causing Louise's cornflakes to slop over the bowl and run on to the floor.

"Now see what you've done," said the caretaker. He went to fetch a mop.

"I'll bet Claude still haunts this place," said Ralph Raven, nudging Stuart Harvey.

"Yeah, when it's dark and everyone's asleep, he'll come creeping in," said Stuart Harvey.

"T O G E T Y O U!" said Ralph, grabbing Louise by the hair.

Louise squealed and this time upset the bowl completely. It shattered on the floor. Mr Sutton, returning with the mop, gave them a murderous look.

"Just clear off," he said.

TUESDAY

Sandra's "Fernlea" Diary

> Mr Sutton, the caretaker, reminds me of one of
> the weasels out of 'Wind in the Willows'.
> He certainly seems a suspicious character.
> Perhaps he isn't really a school caretaker at all,
> but part of a gang on the look-out for children
> to kidnap. Who could he be after? I wonder
> if he'd be interested in Ralph Raven. We
> might be able to do a deal with him.

At 9.30 Year 6 assembled outside the hostel. They were going on a visit to a disused lead mine. By now, Monday's drizzle had turned to a steady downpour. When they reached the mine, the caves were already running with muddy water. It was extremely cold and the few dim lights only made the dark corners more threatening. The noise of dripping water seemed to be magnified. Every shriek and squeal echoed round the caves, surprising even the person who had made it. No one was listening to Mr Mills trying to make himself heard over the noise. Those at the back were busy pushing each other under the heavier showers, as they splashed off the rock face.

Louise was tired and homesick. Mr Sutton's story had not cheered her up. The occasional drops of water, which found their way inside her coat, were like someone's wet fingers reaching down her back. She was glad when the rest of the class began to move out of the cave ahead of her. A narrow passageway forced them into single file. Jane walked in front of Louise. But she turned quickly, when a strangled scream came racing out of the dark. She saw Louise peer anxiously behind her, stumble and lose her footing. Louise slid along the greasy, glistening rocks, and landed in a murky puddle. In the chaos that followed, two shifty characters crept quietly off in the darkness. They stuffed their hands in their mouths, to avoid laughing out loud and giving themselves away.

The girls sat in silence on the coach. Louise looked as if she had been in a fight. Her face was filthy. Her new cream anorak was streaked with green slime.

The coach windows were steamed up. The smell of damp anoraks and fish-paste sandwiches mingled in the air, putting off all but the most determined eaters. Louise opened the half-window above her head. She threw pellets of sandwich to the seagulls which, like Stuart Harvey, seemed to be able to smell food from miles away. She reached in her pocket for a handkerchief, to wipe her fingers. In it she found a piece of paper screwed into a tight ball. She smoothed out the creases and read the words, "WATCH OUT FOR CLAUDE!'

The girls glanced across the bus, to where Ralph Raven and Stuart Harvey were trying to look innocent. They were not very convincing.

"I don't know which would be worse," said Jane, sympathetically, "being half-strangled by a ghost, or having Ralph Raven's clammy hands round your neck." As Cheryl was fond of telling them, there were some things, even in nature, which were beyond the wildest imagination, and Ralph Raven was a good example.

When they got back to the hostel, Mr Sutton was waiting to supervise their entrance. He had laid sheets of newspaper all over the hallway.

"Wipe your feet, leave your boots in the hall and don't drip in the dormitories," he repeated over and over again.

"It's already dripping in our dormitory," Cheryl complained, under her breath. She had been kept awake half the night by the plink! plonk! of rain hitting the bucket. It was like some kind of torture.

She wouldn't have put it past Mr Sutton to have set it up on purpose.

That night, the girls' gang lay awake entertaining each other with jokes and riddles. There was a faint rustling sound, as a white object slid under the door and came to rest in the middle of the floor. Jane turned on the light. She picked up the note. It had Louise's name on the outside.

"I bet it's a love-letter," said Sandra. Inside were the words, "CLAUDE IS COMEING!!"

"You'd have thought a headmaster could spell better than that," said Cheryl. They all laughed at the stupidity of boys in general and Ralph Raven in particular. Only Louise couldn't completely enjoy the joke. She didn't like the way the notes were always addressed to her. It didn't seem fair.

WEDNESDAY

Jo's "Fernlea" Diary

> Last nite a lot of peepol were sik.
> I think it was the fish sandwitches.
> Sturt Arvey was sik in the doorway.
> What a mess! Mr Sutton was mad.
> He said you might eat like a pig but
> theres no need to behayve like won.

On Wednesday morning, Year 6 visited a castle. They were far more interested in the dungeons than any of the upper rooms, which had been carefully restored. Most people secretly hoped that, by a remote chance, someone might get locked in and left behind. If a vote had been taken, it would have probably been a close race between Miss Williams and Ralph Raven.

That night, when the girls were getting ready for bed, Louise found another message under her pillow. It read, "CLAUDE WILL GET YOU!" It had been written in red felt pen. There were little daggers, dripping blood, and ghosts in each corner. Despite the girls' laughter, Louise still felt uneasy. When they were in bed, they took it in turns to tell jokes to try to cheer her up.

"Me first," said Jo. "What should you do if you find a gorilla in your bed?"

"Sleep somewhere else?" said Cheryl.

"What should you know if you want to be a lion-tamer?" said Sandra.

"A little more than the lion," said Jane.

"What did the daddy ghost say to the baby ghost?" asked Cheryl.

"Spooooooook when you're spooooooooken toooo," said Sandra.

"Whoooooooooooooooooo! Whoooooooooooooooooooo! Whoooooooooooooo!"

The sound seemed to go on and on, echoing

around the room, as if people were taking it up and passing it between them like a parcel.

"Don't keep doing that," said Louise. "I don't like it."

The room was very quiet and Sandra's voice seemed to travel a long distance before it reached her.

"But I didn't do it. That wasn't me."

The girls lay quite still in their beds. Jane could feel Louise holding her breath, in the bunk beneath her. Just as each of the girls had managed to persuade herself she had imagined it, the low wailing started up again. Then there was the faint squeaking of hinges.

The door began to open. Next came the soft sound of cloth moving. A vague white shape, the size of a small horse, appeared in the doorway. There was a long intake of breath, followed by, "Whoooo-whoooowhoooo." The shape lurched forward into the room. Louise started to scream. "Whatever it was" left the room in a hurry, banging into the end of the single bed. "OOOOOOYA!" it said, and then pulled the door closed after itself. There was a noise, remarkably like laughter, as it stumbled off down the corridor.

The other girls whispered, "Shshshsh!" in chorus, to try to quieten Louise. But a moment later the door opened and this time the room was flooded with light. The others instinctively hid under the bed-clothes. Miss Williams stood in the doorway, wearing a pink nylon dressing-gown. She was waiting for an explanation.

Jane spoke up quickly. "Louise thinks she's going to be sick . . . any minute."

Miss Williams looked horrified.

"Well, get along to the toilet, child. There's no need to scream and wake everyone up. Jane, go along with her. I'm sure she doesn't need me to hold her hand." As she left, she added, "you could always use that bucket, in an emergency." The bucket, silenced by the weather, had been pushed into a corner, as if in disgrace.

Louise was shivering in the girls' washroom.

"Can't we go back to bed yet? I'm freezing," she said.

"Hang on a minute. We ought to pretend you've been sick," said Jane.

"Don't you think it'd look better if you actually were sick?" said Sandra.

"No," said Louise.

"You could stick your fingers down your throat, like this."

"No," said Louise.

"I could stick my fingers down your throat."

"No!" said Louise.

"Shshsh!" said Jane. She was standing behind the door, peeping into the corridor. She was looking for any signs of life from the boys' dormitory. Not a sound reached her. It seemed as if they were the only people awake in the hostel. But in the boys' bedroom, by the light of a bicycle lamp, Ralph Raven and Stuart Harvey were telling the other boys a rather exaggerated version of what had just happened. It featured themselves, as the intrepid heroes of the tale.

THURSDAY

Jane's "Fernlea" Diary

I'm glad Mr Mills said these were private diaries. That means I can write whatever I like. It's funny how you think you know all about someone until you have to sleep in the same room with them. Then you really find out who snores and who talks in their sleep and who hides a bit of old baby blanket under their pillow.

After breakfast on Thursday morning, the girls returned to their bedroom. There was yet another message. It had been written on the mirror, in soap. In large, clumsy letters it said, "CLAUDE WILL GET YOU . . . TONIGHT!"

"OK," said Sandra. "We'll be ready for them"

"They won't catch us out this time," said Cheryl.

During the morning, Year 6 visited the local church. The vicar showed them round. He was quite unused to talking to young people. He told them all far more than they wanted to know. But after an hour their patience was rewarded. He took them in two groups, to the top of the church tower. They stood windblown, looking out across the countryside, trying to recognize the places they had visited. Ralph Raven edged up to Louise and whispered in her ear,

"That's where he fell . . . SPLAT . . . to the ground. Poor old Claude."

Since it was their last night at the hostel, everyone was late to bed. Mr Mills had organized some entertainment and the girls offered to do one of their plays. It was about a gang of female pirates who terrorized sailors on the high seas. Sandra, of course, played the captain. She managed to have a wooden leg, a hook, one eye and scars all over her face. Her language made both the teachers raise their eyebrows, but, as it was the last night, Mr Mills decided to let it pass.

Back in the dormitory, the girls' gang quickly got ready for bed. Then they constructed an obstacle course, just inside the door. They used their cases, carefully balanced in a pyramid. Any uninvited visitors were bound to walk into it and make a lot of noise. This would give the girls a chance to get out of bed and catch them red-handed. They lay awake, waiting for something to happen. It was getting late and they had already woken Jo twice.

"I wasn't asleep," she insisted. "I was only dozing."

All their attention was concentrated on the door and the corridor beyond it. Any moment they expected to hear the door handle turn. They strained their ears for the slightest sound.

But tonight the boys had another plan of action. They were coming in an entirely different direction. Outside, under the girls' bedroom window, Stuart Harvey was giving Ralph Raven a leg up into the horse-chestnut tree which grew close to the back wall of the hostel. It was a big tree and Ralph needed a lot of help. The trunk was smooth and it was quite a distance before the first branches.

"Push a bit harder, 'Arvey," said Ralph.

"I'm doing the best I can, but you're flaming heavy."

At last Ralph caught hold. Struggling under his own weight, he pulled himself up. After that it was easy climbing. He edged out on to a branch, level with the girls' bedroom window. At a stretch he could tap, with a stick, against the glass.

Down below Stuart Harvey was getting cold. Both boys had pulled sweaters over their pyjamas, but it was a frosty February night. Stuart's legs began to shake.

"Hurry up," he called to Ralph. But Ralph was enjoying himself too much to notice. He reached out his stick. Tap . . . tap . . . tap. Then tap . . . tap . . . tap. "Let me in," he moaned. "Who-ooooooooo. Claude's come to see you." Ralph flapped his arms a bit, ghost-like. There was no one to appreciate this little touch, but it made him feel more the part.

"Whoooooooooooooooooooo!"

"Come on," called Stuart Harvey, "that's enough. I'm getting cold."

At that moment two things happened to spoil Ralph's enjoyment. The first thing was this: Jane, who had quickly realized what was going on, crept out of bed. She peeped from behind the curtain. Ralph's face gleamed at her in the moonlight.

"Louise," she whispered, "get that plastic bucket."

Louise stumbled about in the dark until she found it.

"It's full of water," she whispered back.

"Exactly," said Jane, "bring it over here."

Jane threw open the window. Just two metres

away was the happy grinning face of Ralph Raven. It didn't look happy for very long.

"Whooooooooooooo! Let me in," it was saying.

"Hello, Claude," said Jane. "We've got a surprise for you. Louise, let him have it."

Then Jane ducked down, as Louise emptied the bucket of water out of the window. Like a sudden, heavy shower of rain, it soaked Ralph to the skin.

"Flaming heck! I'm wet through," he hissed at them. There was a clattering as something hit the ground.

In her excitement Louise had let go of the bucket too. The girls crowded to the window to watch, as Ralph, cursing and dripping, made his escape through the branches. He slithered a little way and then hung there, waiting for some help to get down.

Unfortunately, Stuart Harvey wasn't there any more. The second thing that had happened was this: Mr Sutton, the caretaker, coming back from the pub, had just turned the corner of the hostel. Stuart Harvey, hearing his footsteps, had fled inside. This left Ralph stuck up the tree. After a couple of hours at the pub, Mr Sutton might never have noticed Ralph, hidden in the branches. But he could hardly miss the sudden shower of rain, and the flying bucket, which appeared to come from one of the girls' bedroom windows.

Ralph hung for a while, pathetically calling out:

"'Arvey, help me. I can't get down." There was no response. He tried to assess the height and his chances of breaking something if he jumped. Suddenly, a large, horny hand gripped him round the ankle.

"Help! Who's that?" Ralph's teeth were chattering, partly from nerves, partly from cold. His wet clothes were sticking to him.

"It's me . . . Claude, come to help you." And the voice made a deep echoing sound, as if it was coming down a long tunnel, or from inside a bucket.

In blind terror, Ralph let go and slid to the ground. There was a large root growing out of the base of the trunk. He banged his head sharply. He scrambled to his feet and rushed inside the hostel. Out of the corner of his eye Ralph glimpsed a huge white shape like a head but without a face. And the low chuckling sound which came from it made his blood run cold.

By hanging out of the window, the girls had been able to watch some of this. They called to Mr Sutton, who waved the bucket at them. Then the girls hurried to their door, to see Ralph as he came down the corridor. They fought with their cases and just as they cleared a way through, a tragic figure came shuffling in, with a bloody nose, and wet clothes dripping on the tiles. He moaned quietly to himself about "Ghosts" and "Girls". He seemed to be trying to work out, in his own mind, which was the worst of the two evils.

"Goodnight," whispered Sandra.

"Whoooooooo. Sleep tight," said Jane.

"Look out for Claude," called Louise.

But Ralph gave no indication that he had even heard them. He walked on, eyes staring in front of him.

"He looks as if he's been sleep-walking," said Jo.

"He looks as if he's seen a ghost," said Louise. And the girls burst into fits of giggles.

FRIDAY

Louise's "Fernlea" Diary

This has been the best week of my life. I loved it.
I could stay here forever. Except I want to see my mum.
I wonder what she will say about the state of my new
anorak. I wish I didn't have to go home just yet.

When the girls came down to breakfast on Friday morning, there was no sign of Ralph Raven, or Stuart Harvey. Mr Sutton was there, looking quite cheerful. He was always happy on a Friday when the school parties went home. Like most school caretakers, he saw children as nothing but a nuisance, cluttering up the place and dirtying the floors. He winked at Louise.

"You look a lot happier than when you arrived," he said.

"Oh, yes," said Louise, smiling. "Now I don't want to go home."

Stuart Harvey didn't even come down for breakfast. He was still in bed, feeling poorly. He thought he might have caught pneumonia. When Ralph came in there were several loud gasps. He had the beginnings of the most impressive black eye they had ever seen. He was sneezing a lot and his nose was running. He sniffed; Ralph never had a handkerchief.

"Come here, Ralph," said Mr Mills, with a weary sigh. "However did you get that eye?" He was prepared to believe almost anything.

"I don't know, Sir."

"What d'you mean, you don't know?" He wasn't prepared to believe that.

"I think, maybe, I fell out of my bunk, in the night."

"You *think* you fell out! Didn't you wake up?"

Ralph felt trapped in a corner. He didn't know what to say next.

"Perhaps I was sleep-walking, Sir, and bumped into the door."

"I despair of you, Raven," said Mr Mills.

"Perhaps, Sir," said Sandra, eyes shining and hands waving dramatically, "Ralph had a bad dream and fell out of his bunk. He went sleep-walking along the corridor. Finding himself outside, under a tree, he began to climb. Suddenly it came on to rain. Ralph fell down the tree and at the bottom he found a ghost, waiting for him. Picking himself up, he staggered back into the hostel, dripping wet. He found his own room and fell into bed, without ever knowing what had happened to him."

Mr Mills was clearly astonished.

"Sometimes, your imagination runs away with you, Sandra. Not even Ralph would be that stupid." Ralph looked thoroughly uncomfortable, but he was saying nothing.

THE SUPPLY
TEACHER

It was a damp Monday morning towards the end of March. Sandra and Jane pressed their noses against the classroom window. They were hoping that Mr Mills, who was always at school by eight o'clock, would call them in to do a job for him. Not that either of the girls liked doing jobs, at home or at school, but today they were cold and bored. The twins were setting off for school earlier these days, to avoid having to watch their baby brother spreading his breakfast rusk around the table and poking it in his ear.

It was difficult for the girls to see inside the classroom, because condensation ran in little rivers down the huge sheets of glass. They assumed that everyone's school was like theirs, dreamed up by some architect who normally designed greenhouses so that they froze in winter and boiled in summer. But now, with all its lights on, the classroom looked inviting. There was no sign of Mr Mills, which was unusual. As they rubbed on the glass, a small patch cleared. Then they saw something much more unusual; Mr Mills' desk was empty.

Mr Mills' whole classroom had an air of chaos about it. But his desk was the spot from which most of the mess radiated. He liked to keep everything he might need during the day on top of it. When he wanted something he would shuffle through the pile until he found it.

"I have my own filing system," he would say with dignity. Very few of the class were impressed by this. Mr Thacker certainly wasn't. From time to time he tried to tidy Mr Mills up, but it had little effect. But on Friday, Mr Mills had felt the first signs of a sore throat. His wife was recovering from 'flu; she had obviously passed it on to him. He had cleared his desk, in anticipation of a couple of days away from school.

At 8.50 the whistle was blown and Year 6 came into school. There was an uncomfortable feeling in the room, the sort of feeling you have when your mother has changed your bedroom furniture round. Everything's still there, but now it seems unfamiliar. Sandra and Jane had already spread the word that something was wrong. People sat in groups, exchanging opinions. As their voices grew louder, an angry face appeared in the room. It was Miss Williams who taught in the next classroom. Miss Williams wasn't the sort of teacher who shouts at children all day. She had no need to raise her voice. One long look from Miss Williams was enough to quieten even Ralph Raven, the loudest boy in the school.

Miss Williams' face made itself heard above the din. It silenced them in a moment. Most of them had passed through Miss Williams' class at some point. They knew every look, every lift of the eyebrow, every flare of the nostril.

"Silence," raised eyebrows commanded.

"Return to your seats," pointed chin insisted.

"Get out your work," said a prolonged stare into the corner of the room.

"That's better," a satisfied nod relented. Miss Williams returned to her room, having quelled them without a word.

The class was still in crushed silence when the headmaster, Mr Thacker, walked in. Behind him was one of those older girls from the Upper School, who came sometimes to help with infant cooking. Or that was what they thought, until Mr Thacker said:

"Good morning Year 6. I am afraid that Mr Mills has 'flu. He will be off school at least a week, probably two. This is Miss Pickles. She will be teaching you while Mr Mills is away."

Ralph Raven sniggered. Stuart Harvey made a disbelieving sound. The boys' opinions were written clearly on their faces.

"Miss Pickles is an experienced teacher," said Mr Thacker. "I'm sure I can rely on you all to be co-operative."

He smiled, without conviction, at the small, young woman and left the classroom, like the gaoler who has just delivered Daniel into the lion's den.

The boys grinned at Miss Pickles and then at each other. It was quite obvious what they were thinking. The girls didn't know what to think at first, but during break they had plenty to say about the new teacher.

"She's so little," said Cheryl. "I bet she only comes up to Ralph Raven's armpit. It must be something in her genes."

Cheryl was keen on science. She read books on evolution and watched David Attenborough, even third and fourth repeats. She was beginning to work out a few theories of her own.

"Oh, I like her jeans," said Louise. "My mum's going to get me a pair of those when she gets paid."

Cheryl looked at Louise and groaned, but couldn't be bothered to explain.

"She's OK," said Jo. "She's weighed up Ralph Raven already."

"I like the way she ignored him, when he offered to get a step-ladder, so she could write on the board," said Jane.

"I think she looks like Joan of Arc," said Sandra.

Sandra saw everyone as characters from books or films. Mr Mills, on his gloomier days, reminded her of Eeyore, the donkey. Mr Thacker, who was rather full of his own importance, bore some resemblance to Toad of Toad Hall. Whenever Sandra read "The Ice Queen" she always pictured Miss Williams' face. In Sandra's imagination, Ralph Raven played many different parts, but, at the moment he was starring as "The Monster from Outer Space".

After break the class were settling down for a T.V. programme. Ralph Raven and Peter Price stood up and started to leave the classroom.

"Where are you two going?" asked Miss Pickles.

"To take the sandwich trays to the hall," said Ralph. "We do it every day, Miss." And he grinned in triumph.

"Not today," said the teacher. "You did no work before break, you're not wasting another lesson.

Someone else can go. You two girls," she said, indicating Cheryl and Jo.

This made Ralph mad. It had taken him most of last term to rescue this favourite job from those wretched twins. He wasn't going to lose it to girls again.

"Oh, Mr Mills let the girls do it, for a week or two. But he had to come back to us in the end, Miss. Girls are too weedy, especially those two."

"All the more reason, then, to give them a bit of practice," she said. Jo and Cheryl left the room smiling. They thought Miss Pickles was pretty clever. Ralph Raven thought she was barmy.

During the afternoon Ralph's opinion was confirmed. He told Stuart Harvey she was stark staring mad when she chose girls to do woodwork.

"Somebody get the first-aid box, quick," he said.

Miss Pickles was particularly interested in environmental studies. She intended to take the class on a nature walk the next day, to collect specimens to study. When they came back, they would need containers to keep things in, so she was busy showing a few girls how to saw pieces of wood and tack them together. Sandra chewed her tongue with concentration, as she drove the saw deeper with each stroke.

"You'll regret it, you know," Ralph said to the

teacher, "when they cut off their fingers and have to be rushed to the hospital. You have to make sure you take the finger with you, you know. You put it in a plastic bag with a couple of ice-cubes. I saw it on the telly."

Nobody bothered to listen to Ralph. But that didn't stop him.

"Mr Thacker won't like it," he said. "He hates being disturbed during the morning. Don't say I didn't warn you."

Miss Pickles thanked Ralph for his advice. Cheryl reminded him that he was the only one in the class this year to have to be taken to out-patients. He had tried to open a tin of glue with a Stanley knife. He had taken his thumb-nail off.

Miss Pickles asked Ralph and Stuart if they would get back to their own job. This was to collect glass jars from around the school and make sure they were spotlesssly clean. Ralph considered this beneath his dignity. He left the jars to soak in the sink, then went prowling about the classroom. Stuart Harvey had found a store of sunflower seeds, meant for the hamster, in the bottom of one. He was busy eating them in the boys' toilets.

"What are we going to collect in these jars?" Ralph asked Miss Pickles.

"Whatever we find: spiders, beetles, worms."

"Are we gonna cut some worms up?" asked Ralph.

"Certainly not," said Miss Pickles. "You don't have to kill something, in order to study it." Ralph was disappointed.

"Is that all we're gonna get, little creepy-crawlies?"

"Perhaps small mammals, as well. I've got special traps, that won't hurt them." She passed one to Ralph, to look at.

"Must be a bit frightening for them, being caught in a little metal box," said Ralph, in a rare display of imagination.

"I wouldn't like it," said Stuart, joining them, brushing seed cases off his sweater as he spoke.

Cheryl had a moment's fantasy about laying and baiting a Stuart Harvey trap. It would be the easiest thing in the world, she thought. He'd go anywhere for a bit of extra food.

The next afternoon Year 6 set off. They were equipped with glass jars, plastic bags and matchboxes. They walked to the edge of the field, then into a little wood which bordered the school grounds on two sides. Beside a narrow stream, a number of rotting trees lay on the ground, teeming with wildlife. The class split up into small search parties. They went in different directions to find anything which moved and could be carried back to the classroom, for closer investigation.

While everyone else looked carefully inside logs and under stones, coaxing out centipedes and wood-lice, Ralph Raven and Stuart Harvey played at big-game hunters. They stalked one or two of the girls, armed with plastic sandwich boxes, apparently intending to carry the girls off in them.

At three o'clock Miss Pickles blew a whistle to round up the class. The only people missing were the two boys. They had climbed a large tree and spent their time throwing things at anyone who passed underneath. They had forgotten where they had left their boxes and jam-jars. They had absolutely nothing to show for their afternoon's search. Fortunately the rest of the class had.

Before returning to school, Miss Pickles showed the class how to bait and set the mammal traps she had brought. They hid them in the long grass beneath the hedge, close to the wood. She gave them a strict warning about not touching the traps. She told them that they must be checked first thing each morning.

Over the week the class made small homes for beetles and bugs of all kinds – those which could be trusted not to eat each other. Between two pieces of glass, some people made a wormery. Miss Pickles sent Ralph and Stuart out to dig around the school for more worms to stock it. They returned after an hour, shamefaced, with two in a tin. Mr Walton, the caretaker, had found them digging up the rose bushes under Mr Thacker's window. They insisted Miss Pickles had told them to do it, but Mr Walton knew the pair of them too well to fall for that story. He stood over them while they repaired the damage.

Watching different insects at close quarters, the other girls began to understand Cheryl's fascination with them. Louise was obsessed with a group of snails she had collected. She gave them names. She insisted that they all had completely different personalities.

"This one's called 'Dora'," she said. "She's a bit dozy. And this one's 'Lightning'. She moves really fast."

"Fast," said Jo. "You call that fast? It's as slow as a . . . snail."

"Well, she is a snail," said Louise, "but compared with the others, she's like lightning."

Sandra had a collection of spiders in different glass jars. She had given them bits of twigs in the hope that they would spin webs. Each day she caught live flies and fed them into the top of the jars. She began to resemble a spider herself. She lurked silently near the windows, a yoghurt pot in her hand, waiting for a fly to settle. As soon as its hairy legs touched the glass, she pounced, trapping it under the pot.

Cheryl and Jane conducted scientific experiments on a collection of woodlice, which they kept in a large fish-tank. They made light and dark areas, then watched where the creatures congregated.

"What do they eat?" asked Jane.

Cheryl looked it up.

"Dead and decaying plant material," she read, "and animal dung, including their own."

"Oh, really," said Jane. "They're worse than Stuart Harvey and I thought he'd eat anything."

Jo had been on a centipede hunt. She was now occupied with trying to measure their speed. They moved a lot faster than Louise's snails. She'd made an elaborate obstacle course and seemed to be training them for a sort of Centipede Superstars Contest. Her main problem was keeping them apart, since she had found out, the hard way, that they had cannibal tendencies.

As the rest of the class became more enthusiastic about their new project, Ralph Raven became more of a nuisance. He upset people's experiments and caused their insects to escape. He was feeling irritable. So he spent his day picking on the girls.

"D'you know how stupid you look, staring into that jam-jar all day?" he said.

Sandra ignored him. She was watching one of her spiders. It had spun a complicated web the day before. Now it appeared to have taken it down overnight. According to Cheryl it had probably eaten it.

"What are you waiting for?" asked Stuart Harvey.

"To see if it'll rebuild its web," whispered Sandra. She didn't want to disturb the spider.

"It won't if it knows you're watching it," said Ralph.

"It probably wants a bit of privacy," said Stuart.

"Instead of being goggled at every minute of the day," said Ralph.

"How would you like it," said Stuart, as both boys stared at Sandra.

"I don't," she said. "Go away!"

The days passed and Ralph's behaviour became more infantile. The first time Louise opened her dinner-box and found two worms crawling over her sandwiches, she got a nasty shock. But the girls soon got used to finding centipedes in their locker-drawers and spiders in their P.E. bags. Everyone, including Miss Pickles, tried to ignore

Ralph. And the thing Ralph hated most was to be ignored.

One morning Louise was making a series of little houses for her snails, using matchboxes and mini cereal packets. Cheryl had pointed out that snails already have their own houses, on their backs, and you call them shells. This didn't discourage Louise in the least. She was lining boxes with moss and leaves. She made small pebble paths, leading up to the door of each. Ralph crept up behind her and lowered a worm inside the collar of her blouse. Louise calmly got up and said to Cheryl:

"Could you just take a look down my back. I think Ralph might have been dribbling."

The harder it was to upset the girls, the more bad-tempered Ralph became.

"I think all this is a stupid waste of time," Ralph grumbled to Stuart Harvey. "It's days since we did any maths or English. It's not fair." Mr Mills would never have believed his ears. "I mean you don't come to school to watch worms, you come to learn, don't you?" he demanded.

Stuart Harvey wasn't sure what he came for, apart from morning-break, dinner-break and calling in the corner-shop on the way home from school. In between he didn't think about it much.

Towards the end of one afternoon, Ralph managed to break the wormery. Soil and worms and broken glass spilled over the classroom floor. Miss Pickles tried to free the wriggling worms, without cutting her fingers. This time, she looked as if she might lose her temper. The people who had spent days studying the worms making their network of tunnels were not pleased either.

"Why are you causing so much trouble?" said Miss Pickles.

The class turned their hostile faces towards Ralph. Even Stuart Harvey had been drawn into a group who were having beetle races. Ralph felt entirely alone. He didn't know what to say. He tried grinning, but this didn't meet with the usual response; no one grinned back.

At home-time, the girls checked their creatures. Then they packed up their science-folders and went home. Jane left her pencil-box on top of her table ready for the morning. Ralph stayed behind after school, offering to put up the chairs and clean the board. The supply teacher thought that, perhaps, she had got through to Ralph at last. She went home feeling she had had a small triumph.

The next morning, after Assembly, Jane opened her pencil-box and found a very dead slug. It had obviously been trapped all night. Before dying of suffocation, it had spread a silvery trail over her felts and pens and pencils. Her rubber was unusable. She had noticed Ralph, earlier, watching her with that silly grin of his. She soon realized what had happened. Jane was the least hasty and hot-tempered of the girls' gang, but she wasn't going to ignore this particularly cruel trick. She walked over to Ralph.

"I want to talk to you, outside," she said. Ralph told her to pick on someone her own size. Jane gripped his arm and led him into the open area, where some of the class were painting.

"What's wrong with you?" she asked him, looking straight into his face.

Ralph grinned.

"Everyone else is really enjoying this project."

Ralph grunted.

"We've only got Miss Pickles for another couple of days."

"Good thing an' all," said Ralph.

"If you don't stop spoiling everything . . ." said Jane.

"Yeah?" said Ralph.

"We might have to put you in a cage, like the other animals. A playpen or something, to keep you out of the way. You're more of a baby than my brother and he's only a year old."

Ralph tried to laugh it off, but Jane stared him

out. When Miss Pickles came into the area, searching for him, he was glad to get away.

"Ralph, will you go and check the mammal traps this morning?" she said. "They should have been done first thing."

Day after day, the traps had been empty and people were beginning to forget about them.

"Be quick, there might be some poor animal inside, desperate for food," she said. Miss Pickles had never trusted Ralph with this job before. But he seemed to have turned over a new leaf, being so helpful after school yesterday.

Ralph went without much enthusiasm. He was in such a bad mood that even getting out of the classroom didn't cheer him up as it usually did.

A few minutes later, Ralph came rushing back in, shaking the box with excitement.

"Miss, we've got something," he yelled. "Quick, Miss!"

Miss Pickles tried to take the box away from Ralph to spare the poor creature being rattled to death. Ralph held on tightly.

"Aw, let me get it out, Miss," he pleaded.

"All right, Ralph," she said, "but it has to be done carefully. It'll move fast. We need a bag to empty it into." She turned to look for a plastic carrier. Ralph's excitement couldn't be contained.

"Don't worry, Miss, I'll be ready for it," he said. "I'm pretty fast myself." He drew back the catch which held the two halves of the box together.

"DON'T OPEN THAT BOX . . ." Miss Pickles shrieked. It was too late. In a fraction of a second, a tiny, dark object shot up in the air. It leapt, like a miniature kangaroo, clear of the desk and landed halfway across the classroom. It headed instinctively for the open area. After it ran Miss Pickles, Ralph Raven and the entire class. They poured out, past the art-benches and the clay-bins. In its confusion it stopped and changed course, then raced in to the next classroom.

Miss Williams was demonstrating handwriting on the blackboard. Her wrist followed the loops and tails in a smooth, flowing action. Her class watched. They concentrated on clutching their pencils, in an unfamiliar grip, which they only ever managed in handwriting lessons. By the time the mouse, the teacher, Ralph Raven and thirty-one other children had passed through her room, Miss Williams had completed a row of perfect "f's". She gazed at the end of the wild procession. Her mouth opened and closed in shocked silence.

Once more, out in the open area, the mouse fled diagonally to the far corner. It stopped between the boys' toilets and the kiln-room. A low work-surface, littered with wet paintings, provided some shelter. It bolted underneath. With nowhere else to turn, it cowered in the corner, its minute body shuddering.

"I'll get it, Miss. Leave it to me. I'm not afraid," said Ralph, leaning forward.

"Be careful, Ralph, it's very frightened," said Miss Pickles. She was far more concerned for the mouse's safety. The mouse and Ralph seemed to eye one another, as if to see who would make the first move. Slowly Ralph crouched down and leaned towards it. The mouse flew forwards and took refuge in the first dark place it could find, Ralph's trouser leg.

Ralph would have done better to stay bent down, but he instinctively stood up, providing the mouse with a clearer run. It scampered up his leg in a spiral. The bump under Ralph's trousers appeared and disappeared, as it rose, like a helter-skelter, in reverse. Ralph panicked.

"Oh, help, get it out," he shouted, "somebody, get it out."

The mouse reached a tighter spot, which stopped its progress. There was now an obvious bulge, under the pocket on Ralph's bottom.

"For goodness' sake, get it out!" Ralph waved his arms wildly.

Jane stepped forward and cupped her hands

around the bump, to stop it from moving up or down.

"Keep still," she ordered Ralph. He was hopping from foot to foot.

"Get it out," he whimpered.

"Come here, I'll do it," said the teacher.

"Oh no, you won't," said Ralph, backing away.

"Don't be silly," said Miss Pickles. "Now, hurry up, or it might well bite . . ."

"Ow-ya! Ow!" yelled Ralph. The mouse, in panic, had sunk its needle-sharp teeth into his bottom.

Miss Pickles took advantage of the situation. She slipped her hand inside the waistband of Ralph's trousers. She pulled out a tiny, quivering brown mouse, with bright, black eyes, as sharp as its teeth. She held it firmly in her hands. All the class crowded round for a closer look. No one took any more notice of Ralph.

"Ohhhh, it hurts, it hurts," he kept on saying.

"Don't be such a baby," said Jane, "or we'll have to give you a dummy." That really hurt Ralph's feelings. It shocked him into silence.

Mr Thacker was not pleased when he had to break off from filling in his end of term forms. He drove Ralph to the Health Centre without a word. The nurse told Ralph to take off his trousers so that she could inspect the bite. He was about to object, but he caught Mr Thacker's eye. She gave him a tetanus injection, which hurt. Then she laughed out loud and said:

"You'll need a new pair of underpants, someone's chewed a hole in these." Ralph felt thoroughly embarrassed. As he walked back into school, everyone was coming out into the playground, for morning-break.

"Let's have a look at your mouse bite," the girls called to him. Ralph blushed and slunk off to the classroom. He'd had more than enough attention for one day.

THE DEN

Most days after school, during the summer term, the girls' gang met in their den. It was an old wooden shed which belonged to Sandra and Jane's grandad. It was tucked away at the back of his allotment. Now that he was getting too old to garden, the allotment was growing wild and the girls had it all to themselves. It was their secret place . . . until the day that Ralph Raven and Stuart Harvey discovered it. After that there was nothing but trouble.

It was the end of lunch-time. Sandra and Cheryl were carrying the sandwich tray back to the classroom.

"Are you coming to the den today," Sandra asked, "or will you be too busy in your laboratory?"

128

For Cheryl's birthday, her mum had bought her a chemistry set. At first, Cheryl's experiments had only produced disgusting smells, which embarrassed her mother when visitors came. But Cheryl had moved on to greater things. Her older sister, Claire, was taking Chemistry GCSE. Sometimes Cheryl borrowed her equipment. Now her mother was beginning to worry that she might blow up the house, with everyone inside it.

"Of course I'm coming," said Cheryl. "Anyway, my mum's banned my experiments for a week, to let the air clear."

"Good," said Sandra, "that means we can all go to the den today."

The girls felt somebody breathing down their necks.

"Do you think you could hold your Mothers' Meeting somewhere else?' said Ralph Raven. "You're blocking the corridor."

"We were trying to have a private conversation," said Sandra.

"About that soppy gang of yours?"

By way of an answer, Sandra gave him one of her looks. She practised them at home, in front of the mirror, every day. This was her "disgusted" look.

"Where do you lot disappear to after school?" Ralph asked.

"Wouldn't you like to know," said Sandra.

"I could guess. You probably get on your broomsticks and disappear in a puff of smoke."

"Then you'd better be more careful," said Sandra, "or we might turn you into a . . ."

"Handsome prince?" suggested Cheryl.

"Make a change from an ugly toad," said Sandra.

Ralph began to make loud croaking noises. He leapt clumsily towards the girls, arms outstretched. His face was pulled back, into a wide toady grin. He showed a number of yellow teeth and a mouthful of fillings.

"Very good, Ralph," said Mr Mills, coming up behind them. "That should really have the girls falling at your feet."

Sandra gave Mr Mills one of her "scornful" looks.

The shed, where the girls met, still contained some rusty garden tools and open bags of peat, but there was enough room for them all to get inside. To make it more comfortable they had each brought things from home. The favourite item was the deck-chair, which Louise's granny had put out for the Scouts' jumble sale. It had orange and green stripes and a little canvas roof, with a fringe, to shade you from the sun. Not that there was much sun in the den, there wasn't even a window. But there was a skylight, in the roof, which could be propped open to let in some light.

Unfortunately, they had nothing reliable to stand on. Cheryl had brought them a card table, covered with green felt, which folded flat. It was not very popular. Mostly it folded itself up when there were things on it, usually their sweets, hurling them into the corners of the shed and the potting compost. Certainly no one was going to trust the table for standing on. So they had to think of another way to reach the skylight.

When the girls weren't making up plays, their other favourite pastime was gymnastics. With Cheryl directing, they soon learned to make a human pyramid. Sandra and Louise made the bottom tier; Jane stood on their knees; then Jo, who could climb like a monkey, scaled up and pushed open the flap.

With a little light coming in, they could admire their handiwork on the walls. They had brightened up the place with pictures, posters of pop-stars and a number of slogans, which they had collected or made up themselves.

Louise had wanted to make up some rules about the use of the den, but the others didn't like this idea.

"We don't want a load of rules. We get enough of that at school," said Jo.

"We only need one," said Cheryl, and the others agreed with that: "No Boys Allowed".

Today the girls were sitting in the den, waiting for Jo. When she arrived, they were going to work out a new play. They were hoping she would bring some sweets with her. She was often late because she had to help her brother, Paul, with his paper round. She used the extra pocket money she earned to buy sweets for the gang. Eating was another of their favourite pastimes.

There was one of the gang's special knocks on the door. A voice, panting, for breath, said "Ghost."

Sandra called through the door, "Give the full password and enter."

"Oh, for goodness' sake, let her in before she passes out," said Jane.

There was a barely recognizable mutter.

"Speak up, I can't hear you," said Sandra.

"Who else could it be?" said Jane.

A very loud and impatient voice bellowed, "Girls ought'a stick together!"

Sandra carefully opened the door. She had to use both hands because it was only fixed by one hinge. If they weren't careful it might fall off altogether.

Jo came in. She glared at Sandra. Her mouth was bulging with a new gobstopper. No wonder they couldn't tell what she was saying, thought Sandra. No one liked to mention the fact that Jo was eating, and they weren't. There was a moment's embarrassed silence, broken only by the sound of gobstopper against teeth.

"You shouldn't run with that thing in your mouth," said Louise. "You might fall and swallow it. Then it could stick in your windpipe and you'd choke to death. My mum says she knows someone who . . ."

"Oh spare us the details," said Jane. Louise's mother's stories could be quite gruesome. She always knew someone who had suffered some appalling accident. But it had drawn Jo's attention to the sweets. She emptied her pockets out on to the table. The girls smiled and helped themselves.

"I had to come round by your house," Jo told Sandra and Jane. "The Toads were in the park and they tried to follow me. Don't worry, I gave them the slip."

Ralph Raven and Stuart Harvey were referred to, by the girls, as "The Toads". For some time they had been trying to find out where the girls met. "The Toads" occasionally hung around with two

133

other boys, Peter Price and Steven Sprigg. They were known as "The Drips". These two were remarkably similar, even though they were not related. They were both thin and pale, with almost white hair.

Jane said, "Those Drips look like some plants I once grew in the airing cupboard, all white and leggy."

Cheryl said, "They remind me of those animals with a funny name, that live in a dark cave in South America." She'd seen it on David Attenborough.

"I wish that was where they did live," said Jo.

All four boys were in their class at school. The girls considered this more than average bad luck.

Quite soon, there was another of their special knocks. The girls looked around in surprise. A strange, high-pitched voice, threatening to burst into laughter, said:

"Girls ought'a stick together."

Sandra swung the door back. It nearly came off in her hand. Outside were "The Toads".

"Girls ought'a be stuck together," said Ralph.

"With Superglue, preferably," said Stuart Harvey.

Both boys were standing in the doorway, grinning. Ralph Raven was wearing his famous denim jacket. He was never seen without it. His mother hated that jacket. She said it was so old, it was only held together by the badges. It had taken him years to get it like that and Ralph thought he looked great in it.

"What do you two want?" said Sandra.

"We thought we'd come and see what you get up to in here." He nosed his way into the shed and Stuart Harvey closed in behind him.

"Oh look, they're playing house," said Ralph.

"Judging by this place, they need all the practice they can get," said Stuart.

"Push off, you two," said Sandra.

"Yeah, get lost," said Jane.

"Make us," said Ralph. Stuart Harvey moved in closer.

The girls looked at each other. The odds were in their favour. They moved forwards, as if by telepathy, pushing their sleeves up, in a gesture the boys easily understood. Ralph nervously stepped backwards; even he could count.

"OK, OK," he said, "but we'll be back and we'll bring reinforcements next time." They rode away on their bikes, singing, "Girls ought'a be stuck together." They wobbled along the path and out towards the recreation field. They turned for a moment to call, "Don't worry, we'll be back."

And they were. Whenever there was nothing

better to do the boys would creep up on the den and bang on the walls, with sticks. Then they would ride around outside, calling out rude remarks.

"It's the Evo-stick gang." And when the girls told them to "Get lost!", they would say, "Don't speak to those girls, they're all stuck up." They laughed loudly at their own jokes, while the girls sat miserably, trying to ignore them, hoping they would go away. For a few days the girls couldn't face going to the den. When they did meet again, they found that the place had been turned upside down.

"Just look at this mess," said Cheryl.

"It's worse than Mr Mills' stock-cupboard," said Jane.

"We've got to do something about those boys," said Sandra.

"They're bigger than us," said Louise.

"But we've got bigger brains," Cheryl reminded them. It was one of Cheryl's scientific theories, that boys actually had smaller brains than girls. Most of Cheryl's theories were based on her own careful observation.

"We must be able to find a way to outwit Ralph Raven," said Sandra.

"That sounds simple enough," said Jane. The girls thought hard. Louise chewed her hair for inspiration.

At last Jo said, "Couldn't you make a bomb, with that chemistry set of yours? We could lock them in here and you could blow 'em up!"

The other girls looked at her pityingly.

"Then where would we meet, Stupid?" said Sandra.

"And what do you think my grandad would say if we blew up his shed?" said Jane.

"It was just an idea," said Jo.

"But we could lock them in here," said Louise, "for a few days. That would teach them a lesson."

"Someone would be bound to hear them and let them out," said Jane.

"Not if we gagged them first." The girls considered this.

"They'd probably die with nothing to eat," said Jane. "Stuart Harvey would for sure."

The girls were thinking of entering Stuart Harvey for the *Guinness Book of Records*. The amount he ate must be some kind of record. Nobody could work out where he put it all. Cheryl's theory was that it went straight to his head and that his brain, already under-developed, was being crowded out by a mountain of rotting food. Judging by some of the stupid things he came out with at school recently, it would soon cease to function altogether.

"If they did die, we'd be stuck with all the bodies," said Jo, in disugst.

"Yes," said Louise, "if we left them here for long, the place would start to smell." The girls held their noses at the thought of it.

"My mum says she knows someone whose uncle was in the First World War, and he told her . . ."

"Oh, give over, I feel sick already," said Sandra. The girls were quiet for a while.

Slowly an evil smile spread over Cheryl's face. "That's it," she said.

The girls' ideas hadn't been practical, but they had given her something to work on. Now she had thought of a very pleasing revenge. The others liked it too.

"If you get them in here and lock them in, I'll take care of the rest," said Cheryl. "It will be quite a challenge."

Every day after school the girls were occupied, making their preparations. Jo borrowed her brother's tool kit and, between them, the girls fixed the hinge so that the door closed properly. She also borrowed Paul's bicycle padlock and chain. Brothers had their uses, sometimes. The girls didn't see much of Cheryl; she was busy in her laboratory. Fortunately, her mum had lifted her ban and she experimented all week. With some help from her sister, Cheryl managed to create what she described as "The Smelliest Stink Bomb in the World".

By Thursday the girls' gang were ready for action. Now they only needed to entice the boys into their den. The boys didn't need much encouragement. The mended door and padlock and chain were enough to arouse their interest. And the girls, who were experts at improvising drama, gave them the final bait. They stood whispering in corners. Whenever the boys appeared, they broke off in mid-sentence, and moved away, whistling.

"What did I tell you?" said Ralph Raven. "Those girls are up to something and we're going to find out what it is."

At six o'clock the boys were spotted cycling towards the den. Sandra and Jane's garden was at the far end of the allotments. From their hiding place, behind the hedge, you could see the shed. Louise, who was looking through her dad's bird-watching binoculars, saw the boys first. Cheryl and Jo were hidden behind some garden sheds further along from the den, near the gate through which the boys were likely to come. They had been hidden for what seemed like hours and they were getting cramp. Cheryl was clutching the precious test-tube, securely closed with a rubber bung. They were both relieved when they heard the sound of bicycle wheels and the familiar voice of Ralph Raven.

"I told you there'd be no one here," said Ralph.

"And they've forgotten to lock up," said Steven Sprigg.

"Just like girls to spend all their pocket money on a padlock and then leave it undone,'" said Peter Price.

"Let's see what the big surprise is," said Stuart Harvey. "I hope it's something to eat. Thursday's my mum's bingo night and I only had fish and chips and a packet of Bakewell tarts, I'm starving."

The boys dropped their bikes on the ground and went into the shed. They didn't suspect a thing. Jo edged nearer and, as the last one was through the door, she sprang forward, closed and locked it, before they knew what had happened.

Cheryl was by Jo's side. The other girls, who had set off at a run, soon joined them. By now the boys were shouting and hammering on the door. They couldn't see the girls outside, but they knew they had been caught. Ignoring the cries and threats, the girls assembled at the end of the shed, ready to put part two of their plan into action.

Fortunately, it was a quiet time for gardeners. Only Mr Moore, a neighbour of the twins, was on the allotment. Straightening up to ease his back, he looked over and watched the girls as they made their pyramid in record time. He watched Jo scale up in a second. He saw Cheryl pass something, with the greatest care, into her hands. He'd often watched the girls and marvelled at their acrobatics. He couldn't make out, this time, why they should be wearing masks, but he'd seen them in far stranger outfits. He chuckled to himself and went back to thinning his carrots.

Clutching the test-tube, Jo checked her mask was tightly in place. She threw open the skylight, flooding the den with light for a moment. She shook the contents of the tube briskly into the shed and slammed the skylight down, before any trace could escape. She flung the empty test-tube, as far as she could, into the shrubs, which edged the allotments. Now that her hands were free, she took the two bricks, which Cheryl passed up to her, and placed them on top of the skylight to weight it down. That should take care of the only possible escape route.

Within seconds, the girls ran clear of the shed. They stayed close enough to see that no one came along and let the boys out. They had reckoned that the plan needed five minutes for maximum effect. It would be a waste of all that planning and practice if the boys escaped too soon. But they were making so much noise. The girls could hear them plainly and they realized that Mr Moore could too. He was looking their way and Sandra decided to go and distract him before he came to investigate. Cheryl was timing the plan on her digital watch.

"You've got to keep him busy for four more minutes," she told Sandra.

Even Sandra, with all her acting ability, found it difficult to cover up the nervousness she was feeling.

"Hello, Mr Moore. Your carrots are very good. They're much better than my dad's."

Mr Moore gazed anxiously over her shoulder.

"There's quite a commotion coming from yon shed. What's to be doing, then? Are you girls up to some'at?"

"It's just four boys from our class. They keep coming and raiding our den . . . so we locked them in . . . to teach them a lesson, you know."

"They're making a powerful lot of noise. What did you put in there with them, a bomb?"

Sandra laughed too loud. "They're probably scared of the dark. They're a pretty wet lot, boys, don't you think?"

Mr Moore looked at her closely and Sandra couldn't hold his eye. She stared at her feet, wondering if four minutes were up yet.

"Perhaps we better let them out," she said.

"Perhaps you better!"

Sandra ran back to the others.

"Hurry up," called Cheryl. "They've had six minutes already. They'll be gassed."

"Well, go and let them out," Sandra shouted back.

Jo raced to the shed, mask tightly over her face. Carefully she unlocked the door. Although the boys had stopped banging on the shed, they were still shouting, but at each other now.

"Trust you to get us into this mess, Raven," said Steven Sprigg.

"My mum's always telling me to keep away from you," said Peter Price. "I wish I'd listened to her."

"It wasn't my fault," Ralph complained. "How was I supposed to know them lousy girls would lock us in."

"If they don't let us out soon," moaned Stuart Harvey, "I could miss my supper."

With the terrible smell in the shed, food was the last thing the other boys were thinking about.

Jo unhooked the padlock and took it with her, running as fast as she could, to join the others in the safety of the twins' garden. They were in position, ready to enjoy the sight of the boys emerging from the shed. They were each trying to coax the binoculars from Louise, to get a better view of the boys' faces.

The door of the shed slowly swung open and the boys tumbled out, coughing and spluttering. According to Louise, their faces were a funny green colour, the shade her dad had painted the outside toilet.

The boys looked around for the girls' gang, searching behind the sheds and then in the hedge which bordered the allotments. They kept one hand over their noses, the free arm waved wildly about, clearly threatening what they would do if they found the girls. At last they gave up the search, collected their bikes and pedalled furiously away from the nauseating smell.

The girls went on watching, for a few minutes, enjoying their revenge. Just then, Mr Moore walked along the central path, carrying his watering-can. The communal tap was quite a distance from the girls' den, but when he reached it, they saw him raise his head, look round in surprise, sniff the air and pull a terrible face.

The next day at school, Mr Mills said, "I don't normally make such personal remarks, but there is a dreadful smell in this room and it does appear to be coming from one particular corner. I think we'd better have the windows opened."

No one would sit near the boys. They didn't want to sit next to each other, but they had no choice.

They glared across at the girls' gang. But whenever they caught the boys looking over, the girls took on expressions of complete innocence. Wide-eyed, open-mouthed, their faces seemed to say, "What . . . us?"

During break, Cheryl overheard Stuart Harvey telling Ralph Raven:

"I got sent straight to bed last night, with no supper. I was starving. My stomach kept me awake for hours."

This met with little sympathy from Ralph.

"That's nothing. My mum went mad. She made me strip off outside the back door and she stuffed the rest of my clothes in the washer. But she took my jacket and told my dad to burn it, on the bonfire. I loved that jacket. Those girls are gonna be sorry," he said.

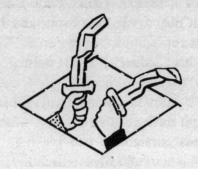

THE SCHOOL PLAY

The girls' gang was really excited. Mr Mills had told them that Year 6 was to put on a play in front of the whole school, at the end of term. The girls' gang was mad about plays; they had been practising them all year. But this one would have scenery and costumes and make-up. Today he was going to tell them about the play and sort out the parts. The girls had come in, specially early, from dinner-break. They sat on the edge of Mr Mills' table, swinging their legs and looking out on to the field.

"I wonder what play we're going to do?" said Sandra.

"I wonder?" said Louise.

"I hope I get a good part," said Sandra.

"I hope I get a good part," said Louise.

146

"I hope it's *Treasure Island*," said Cheryl, "then Sandra can play Long John Silver and Louise can play the parrot."

"I hope it's *Cinderella*," said Louise.

"Yukkk!" said the others.

"We don't want that wet story," said Jo.

"We want some good strong parts with plenty of action," said Sandra.

"I like *Cinderella*," Louise insisted.

"But she's such a twit," said Jane, "letting those two boss her around. And what does she get in the end? Nothing."

"She gets to marry the prince," said Louise.

"Exactly," said Jane, "talk about the booby prize."

Louise had been in the girls' gang nearly a year but sometimes, even now, the other girls despaired of her. Jane blamed it on those comics she read. Louise believed in all that romantic rubbish. Cheryl said Louise's brain was like a piece of blotting paper, it would soak up anything. Louise wished it would soak up her eight times table. They were having a test tomorrow and she couldn't seem to keep it in her head.

"Anyway," said Jane, "think who you might get for the prince."

The girls' gang looked out of the classroom

window. Some of the Year 6 boys were coming in from the field: Michael Flynn and Anthony Kariolis clutching their chess set, Steven Sprigg, Peter Price, Stuart Harvey, it got worse and worse. Last of all, the ultimate horror, Ralph Raven. Even Louise would have burned at the stake, rather than hold hands with Ralph Raven.

Throughout the year, Ralph had been their biggest enemy. It had been one long battle. But after the summer holidays, they would be moving on to the High School into different classes. At last they might get rid of him. Occupied with this happy thought, the girls didn't really notice Ralph. But he saw them, gazing towards him, smiling to themselves. He gave them a condescending wave. Then he winked at them. There was still no reaction. Ralph came close to the window and gave them a big, smacking kiss. It left a wet ring on the glass. Suddenly they saw him. Sandra clutched one hand to her mouth, the other to her stomach. She rolled off the desk and on to the floor, groaning. The other girls followed her, like a pack of cards, until all five were doubled up, moaning and pretending to be sick. Ralph stared at them, his mouth wide open. Mr Mills walked into the room and saw Ralph, framed in the glass, behind his desk.

"Come on, girls. He's not that bad."

Ralph, sensing he was being talked about, broke into a wide, idiotic grin and waved. Mr Mills began to see their point.

"Get in here, Ralph," he said. "We've got a lot to do this afternoon."

After the register had been found, behind the fish tank, and filled in, the class looked expectantly at Mr Mills.

"We're going to do a play, about St George and the Dragon,'" he announced.

"Great!" said the boys. They knew there would be some good fighting in it.

"Mmmmm," said Melissa Whitehead, the prettiest girl in the class. She knew there would be a princess in it.

"Hummph," said the girls' gang. They could see nothing in it for them.

"Just great," Cheryl grumbled. "The boys'll get the best parts, Melissa Whitehead'll be the princess, and we'll be left as the trees."

"Oh, don't be silly," whispered Sandra. That kind of thing happened in Year 1, but not in Year 6. Surely!

Once the boys had been sorted out, Mr Mills began to look uncomfortable.

"Now, er, I'm afraid there are not many girls in this play, apart from the princess, of course. I thought Melissa would make a good princess."

Melissa pretended to blush and seem surprised. The girls' gang were not impressed by her acting.

"But we shall want some villagers," he said, glancing hopefully at the girls' gang. Sandra was deeply insulted. "And the rest of the girls are going to do a dance with Miss Williams."

"What sort of dance?" asked Sandra.

"Er, some group work," he said vaguely. He tried to give the impression it was nothing to do with him. "They're going to be . . . er . . . plants and trees and things."

The girls' gang showed what they thought of that idea.

"Miss Williams has been on a dance course and she's very keen." Mr Mills didn't need to say any more. If Miss Williams was keen, it would be like trying to resist a bulldozer. The girls spent the rest of the afternoon sulking.

At home-time Sandra was in a real temper.

"Sir, I don't think it's fair to give all the best parts to the boys."

"Now, Sandra," said Mr Mills. "We can't please everyone."

He searched his pockets for his car keys. He was in a hurry to get off to the dentist. Jane found them by the blackboard.

"But I'd like to have been St George," said Sandra.

Mr Mills disappeared out of the room.

"You!" hooted Ralph Raven. "Don't be stupid."

"I could do it as well as a boy," she said, raising herself to her full height.

"You couldn't act your way out of a paper-bag."

This was the cruellest thing he could have said to Sandra.

"I should stick to waving your branches," said Ralph, his arms flapping by his sides. "At least playing a tree should keep you quiet."

For once Sandra was speechless. She gave Ralph a look of pure poison.

The next week rehearsals began. Each afternoon Year 6 went along to the Hall. When they reached the Hall door those with main parts went inside, while the "trees" stayed in the cloakroom. They were supposed to practise their dance and keep themselves occupied until Miss Williams was free to work with them. Michael Flynn and Anthony Kariolis had no interest in plays or sword-fighting. They were considered hopeless cases, as far as plays were concerned, so they were allowed to sit on the benches, under the coat hooks, playing endless games of chess. Apart from chess, they never wanted to do anything. Cheryl had often wondered at how anyone could have so little interest in living, and still bother to breathe.

There were a few girls who took the dancing seriously. They curved and twisted around the coat stands, waving their arms up and down. The girls' gang gave them looks which would have withered full-grown trees. The dancers went off to find a more sympathetic audience.

The girls' gang sat side by side on the bench.

"I'm really bored," said Jo. She could begin to see how someone might die from the complaint.

"It's not fair!" said Sandra.

"Oh, let's do something instead of moaning," said Cheryl.

"Like what?" said Jane.

"We'll do our own play," said Cheryl. "Nobody'll even notice, as long as we keep Sandra quiet." Sandra gave Cheryl an "offended" look.

"What play?" asked Jo, irritably.

"Well, we need to find a play with five good parts for girls," said Cheryl.

That sounded pretty unlikely. They were usually lucky to come up with a play with one strong female character, but five . . . they thought of all the popular stories they knew. In every case, the girls had the worst of the bargain. They were always getting locked up or put to sleep, then having to wait around for years, until some prince turned up. Even worse, they spent most of the story doing housework, like Cinderella, or cooking for a gang of dwarfs, like Snow White. The witch was the only one with any spirit and she usually came to a sticky end.

"The boys get the best of everything," grumbled Jo.

"Yes," agreed Sandra. "Look at Mr Mills' play, I'd have liked to be the knight."

"So, we'll make up our own play and you *can* be the knight."

"We could call it, *St Georgina and the Dragon*," said Jane.

"Mmmm," said Sandra. That sounded quite a promising start. Then everyone else wanted to choose their favourite character and soon things began to get out of hand.

"I shall be a wicked witch," said Jo, "that turns everyone into toads and treads on them." She leapt up and stamped viciously on the ground.

"I want to be Wonder Woman," said Louise, firmly.

"What about the princess?" said the others.

"She'd only be a wet and who wants to be a wet?" Perhaps Louise was changing after all.

"I shall play Doctor Her, a famous scientist," said Cheryl.

"You mean Doctor Who," said Jo.

"No, I don't," said Cheryl. "This one will be female so, obviously, twice as clever."

'Right, Jane, that means you'll have to be the dragon," said Sandra.

"Oh no, I won't," said Jane.

"We still need a wet princess," Jo suggested, "to rescue from the dragon."

"If I play the princess," said Jane, "she won't be wet and she won't need you lot to rescue her. She'll be able to look after herself."

The gang sat stubbornly, glaring at one another. The girls had each chosen their parts and they weren't prepared to give them up. If the chess players had been at all interested, they would have recognized this as "stale-mate". It wasn't going to be easy; working out a story around a knight, a bossy princess, a bad-tempered witch, Wonder Woman and a female Doctor Who. It sounded almost impossible. The girls' gang knew they would eventually sort something out. But at the moment they still didn't even have a dragon.

"It's going to be a pretty stupid play without a dragon of some kind," said Sandra.

"Can't we manage without a dragon for now?" said Jo, keen to get started.

"It could be a cowardly dragon, that stays inside

its cave for most of the play," said Cheryl.

"So we'd only need someone to roar, now and again," said Jane.

"They wouldn't need to be good at acting," said Louise.

"They wouldn't need to be any good at anything," said Jo.

The girls glanced across at the two boys, playing chess. The part might have been written for them.

"Do you think you could help us out, by roaring?" said Sandra.

"You know, like a dragon," said Jane.

Neither boy raised his eyes from the chess-board. They weren't much interested in roaring.

"Do you know how to roar?" Sandra persisted.

The boys nodded. Anything for a quiet life.

"Well, go on then."

"Hrrghow," said the boys, half-heartedly.

"That was pathetic," said Sandra. "It sounded like a frog with a sore throat. Look, like this." She threw back her head and opened her throat. Jane realized too late. She clapped her hand over Sandra's mouth. But the sound had already escaped. It shook the glass in the Hall door and actually moved a vase of flowers a little way along the radiator shelf. Mr Thacker's door opened.

"Now see what you've done," said Jane. "You and your voice."

A couple of days later the girls were in their den, rehearsing for the play. They had been working very hard because they wanted this play to be perfect. But at the moment there was still a lot of disagreement about the plot.

"If you ask me," said Sandra, "it's a funny sort of play where the main character spends most of it stuck to the spot."

She had just been put under a spell, by Jo, playing the witch. Drunk with her own power, Jo was now doing cartwheels round her victim, cackling in triumph. Sandra considered this a stupid way to play the part. Whoever heard of an acrobatic witch?

"It doesn't need to stop you from speaking," said Cheryl. "I don't come on until nearly the end and I'm not complaining."

"But I'm supposed to be the hero," said Sandra, throwing her sword to the floor.

"Heroine," Jane corrected her. Jane was also sulking. Sandra had tied her to a tree. She was expected to stay there for the rest of the play and she didn't like the idea.

"This is the only fair way of working it out," said

Cheryl. "If we let you kill off the dragon, there'll be nothing for the rest of us to do."

"And we all want to have a go at the dragon," said Jo.

"What dragon?" said Sandra, sharply. "We don't have a dragon yet, in case you've forgotten."

The girls sat and thought about all this. Although they each felt their own role in the play wasn't as much as their talents deserved, they could see Cheryl's point. They wanted it to be fair. And Sandra was right, too. They *had* to find a dragon from somewhere. Whoever could be persuaded to play the part, knowing the fate they had planned for it?

"What we need," said Cheryl, "is someone really big."

"With a deep voice," said Jo.

"Masses of acting ability," said Sandra.

"But stupid enough to go along with the ending," said Jane.

"Or stupid enough to be tricked into the ending," said Cheryl.

"But do we know anyone that stupid?" said Jane. The girls began to smile.

"He'd never agree to it," said Jo.

Sandra, still smarting from Ralph's cruel insults, began to see a chance for revenge.

"Oh, but he might," she said. "He just might."

The following Monday it poured with rain and Year 6 had to stay inside at break-time. The windows were misted up and people played noughts and crosses on them. The air in the room was heavy and damp. The noise level rose as voices tried to cut through it, like blunt scissors. Mr Mills sat at his desk, clutching his cup of coffee, marking maths books. Two girls tidied his desk around him.

Ralph Raven was sitting at his table, drawing a Dangermouse cartoon.

"That's great," said Sandra, sitting on the corner of his table.

Ralph leaned forward, edging her off with his elbow.

"You're really good at drawing," said Jane. It was true, but difficult to admit.

"And you're good at acting," said Cheryl.

"Have you thought about going on the stage, when you grow up?" said Louise.

Ralph narrowed his eyes. He glanced from one girl to another.

"What you after?" he said.

"Nothing," said Sandra.

"Well then, clear off."

"To tell you the truth, we were wondering whether to offer you the star part in our play."

"Don't bother," said Ralph.

"It's a good part," said Jane.

"What play?" said Ralph.

"It's a bit like Mr Mills' play," said Cheryl. "Knights and dragons, but ours is better."

Ralph was unconvinced.

"In our play," said Sandra, "the best part isn't the knight, it's the dragon."

"And we thought you'd make a brilliant dragon," said Jane.

"We need someone with a powerful voice," said Jo.

"Someone who can act," said Sandra.

"Someone intelligent," said Louise.

Ralph stopped drawing. He smiled to himself and puffed out his chest.

"This dragon," he said, "what does he have to do?"

The girls relaxed a little. They could see he was hooked.

"He has to roar a lot," said Jane.

"Is that it?"

"Oh no," said Sandra. "He has this big role to play, at the end."

"Does he get to eat you all up, then?" he asked, grinning unpleasantly.

"Oh yes," lied Sandra. She crossed her fingers behind her back. "He's the real hero. We just roll over and die."

The other girls blushed at the outrageous lies they'd been telling. However were they going to get round the last one?

"Well, I'll think about it," said Ralph, playing hard to get.

"Great!" said Sandra. "You won't regret this."

"Hmmm," said Ralph, a small doubt stirring in his mind.

Looking up from his desk, Mr Mills saw the extraordinary sight of the girls' gang in some sort of agreement with Ralph Raven. He shivered at the thought. There were only two weeks left until the end of term; surely nothing too awful could happen in that time. But the girls had been unusually quiet. He had an idea they might be planning something, a sort of final surprise. The prospect made Mr Mills feel suddenly weary.

The next day, during the dinner hour, the girls' gang and Ralph Raven were behind the coke store. They were explaining what they wanted him to do. He was not being very co-operative.

"You mean to say I spend most of the play hiding at the back of a cave? I thought this was supposed to be a good part."

"Look, it's important. Just because the audience can't see you doesn't mean you can go to sleep," said Cheryl.

"You have some important roars," said Sandra.

Ralph was fed up already, and he showed it.

"If it's too difficult," said Jane, "we could always find someone else."

"Never mind, get on with it," he said. He wasn't that fed up, yet.

"You have to roar in all the right places," said Jo.

"You'd better give me a copy of your lines," said Ralph, wearily.

"Oh, we haven't got any lines," said Cheryl. "We make them up as we go along."

"So how . . . do I know . . . when to roar," said Ralph, as if speaking to an idiot, "when I'm stuck at the back of the cave?"

"I'll poke you," said Cheryl.

"You can clear off," said Ralph. He'd had enough of these girls.

"Let's have a practice," said Jane, quickly. They got into their places. Ralph crouched in a corner, behind the dustbins. Cheryl prodded him in the back.

"UHGHHHHHH RRRRRR OOOOWW WWWWWGH HGHGHGHGHGH!" It went on and on.

"All right, all right, that's enough. We'll never get through it at this rate," said Cheryl. But Sandra was impressed. Ralph's roar had brought two dinner ladies and several infants rushing over to see who was being murdered. Nevertheless, she realized it was going to be difficult controlling Ralph's enthusiasm. Not to mention the problem of what to tell him about the ending. As if reading her thoughts, Ralph said:

"When can we practise the bit where I come out?"

"Oh, there's plenty of time for that," said Sandra, uncomfortably. "We'll do your bit tomorrow." She was still saying that, at the end of the week, and Ralph was getting impatient.

Fortunately, it was close to the performance of Mr Mills' play which was fixed for the following Monday afternoon. This helped to keep Ralph rather busy. He was playing a knight, who had a vicious sword-fight with Stuart Harvey, another knight. Judging by the number of broken swords the acting must have been very convincing. Mr Mills prayed each day that they would reach Monday without anyone damaging themselves. Two people had dropped out, after complaints from their mothers about bruises and ripped sweaters. Even some of the boys themselves thought it was getting a bit rough.

Miss Williams had thrown the girls' gang out of her dance group. It had proved impossible to prevent Jo from uprooting herself and going for a walk-about whenever she felt like it.

"For goodness' sake, child, you're supposed to be a living tree," said Miss Williams. "You look as if you've been struck by lightning."

Jo had become bored with practices. She was doing handstands against the kiln-room door. And the other girls had lost interest too. One afternoon Miss Williams chopped them down with some sharp glances and equally cutting remarks.

"We've got far too many trees," she said. "Let's get rid of the dead wood. You five . . . can go!"

The girls didn't mind in the least. It gave them more time to devote to their own rehearsals.

On Monday, *St George and the Dragon*, Year 6's play, was performed in the Hall, for the rest of the school. The girls' gang agreed it was "OK", but they thought there was too much fighting. It looked to them like a good excuse for the boys to try to chop off each other's heads. Year 1 had loved it. Mr Mills was relieved that everyone had escaped unhurt. Next year, he thought, he would choose something a little less violent: *Cinderella* or *Snow White*, a play with nice parts for the girls.

It was the end of the afternoon. Mr Mills was

sitting at his desk relaxing. Only four days left to the end of term. The girls' gang gathered around him.

"Sir, are you in a good mood?" Sandra asked. Mr Mills hated those words. In his experience, they always meant trouble.

"Why?"

"Well, it's like this, Sir, we were wondering whether . . ."

Mr Mills hadn't the heart to refuse. It was decided that the girls' gang, with Ralph Raven as the dragon, would perform their play for the rest of the class on Thursday, the day before the end of term. They assured him it was well-organized. All they needed from him were one or two school costumes. And for some reason he couldn't begin to fathom, the use of the scramble net. It was lying, gathering dust, in a corner of the classroom. It hadn't been put away from Sports Day.

On Wednesday, Ralph was still asking the girls when they were going to work on his last scene.

"We haven't done my bit yet," he reminded them.

"Don't worry about it," said Cheryl.

"What's there to practise?" said Jo. "You come out, we roll over and die, and you get the applause."

"You'll know what to do, when the time comes," said Sandra.

"OK," said Ralph, shrugging his shoulders. He was planning a long drawn-out scene for himself, where he mangled and chewed them to death. He would walk all over them, if he felt like it. He was quite looking forward to it. He could already hear the cheers and the applause. It would be a good chance to get his own back on those wretched girls. Goodness knows he'd had enough to put up with from them during the year. This would be his final revenge.

That night, the girls met in their den to have a last run-through. Ralph had not been invited.

"Are you sure this is going to work?" said Louise.

"'Course it will," said Sandra. "Why shouldn't it?"

"He won't know what's hit him," said Jane.

"He's not going to take it quietly," said Jo.

"Yes, but there's five of us," said Cheryl, "and we'll have the element of surprise."

"He'll be so mad," said Jo, grinning.

"Serve him right," said Jane. "Think of what we've had to put up with from him this year."

The girls sat, for a moment, remembering some of those times. Yes, they each thought, this would show Ralph Raven once and for all. This would be their final revenge.

After lunch on Thursday, the girls set out their scenery and props. Ralph was being quite helpful. He seemed nearly as excited as the girls. Even Sandra felt a twinge of guilt, but it was too late now. The rest of Year 6 were coming in, giggling and pink-faced. They sat, then swopped seats and nudged each other in anticipation.

"All right, settle down," said Mr Mills. "Stuart Harvey, put those sweets away, this isn't a cinema."

At last everyone was ready. Sandra stepped forward, dressed as a knight. She proudly announced,

"St Georgina and the Dragon, A One-Act Play by The Girls' Gang, including Ralph Raven as the Dragon Damselslayer."

And the play began.

THE PLAY

ST GEORGINA
AND THE DRAGON

Cast List

ST GEORGINA	Sandra Turner
PRINCESS JASMINE	Jane Turner
WILHELMINA, WITCH OF THE WOODS	Jo Robson
WONDER WOMAN	Louise Bottomley
DOCTOR HER	Cheryl Spencer
THE DRAGON DAMSELSLAYER	Ralph Raven

The play is set on the edge of a deep, dark wood, at the foot of a hill. In the side of the hill is the mouth of a cave. Around the cave, the ground is littered with bones (which the girls have been begging from the butcher for the last two weeks). There are a few trees with burnt branches. From time to time, a low roaring can be heard from the depths of the cave. "RRAAAARRRRRRRGHGHGH." Close by the cave a Princess is leaning against a tree, carving a piece of wood with a penknife.

A Knight in shining (cardboard) armour approaches riding a horse (Louise's sister's hobby-horse). She is carrying an enormous sword, which trails on the ground. She dismounts, leaving her horse (propped up like a bike) against another tree.

KNIGHT: Have no fear, sweet Princess, your Knight in shining armour is here. I have come to rescue you from the wicked dragon and save you from a terrible fate. *The Knight bows.*

(Sandra is unable to bend, because her armour cuts into her stomach. She groans. "Get on with it," Jane whispers.)

Do not faint or weep, Princess. Do not beat your breast.

(This causes giggling among the audience. Sandra gives them a "disgusted" look.)

Do not fall to your knees and kiss my feet.

PRINCESS: Don't worry, I won't.

KNIGHT: Be of good cheer. I am St Georgina and I
have come to free you, dear damsel in distress.

PRINCESS: Save me? There's really no need.

KNIGHT: Are you not the Princess Jasmine,
daughter of the King of this land?

PRINCESS: Yes, I am.

KNIGHT: And have you not been abandoned here?
Doomed to be eaten by the dreadful Dragon,
known in these parts by the name of "Damselslayer"?

There is a loud roar, "HHRRAAAARRGH-
GHGHGH!" It sounds as if the Dragon is saying,
"That's me they're talking about."

PRINCESS: What if I have? It's nothing to do with
you.

KNIGHT: Are you not afraid? A helpless young girl
left here to be devoured by this mighty monster. Forgotten, forsaken, forlorn.

PRINCESS: Afraid? Certainly not. What kind of a weakling do you think I am?

KNIGHT: Brave words, Princess. *The Knight claps the Princess on the back.*

(She claps her a little too hard, so Jane hits her back. For a moment, it looks as if there might be a fight.)

PRINCESS: Anyway, who are you?

KNIGHT: Allow me to introduce myself. I am St Georgina, famous, female, "Rent-A-Knight". I am at the service of helpless maidens, twenty-four hours a day. "Dragons Slayed, Monsters Murdered, Princesses Preserved." Please accept my card.

PRINCESS: *She tears up the card and throws it over her shoulder.* Just get lost, will you? I'm not a "helpless maiden". You're out of date. Us modern girls have learnt to take care of ourselves. We don't scare easy.

(In the background, a jab from Cheryl produces a particularly loud roar, which echoes around the stage, "HRHRAAARRRGHGH!" Behind the scenes, Cheryl hisses, "That's enough!" The roaring stops.)

The Knight lifts her sword and points it towards the cave.

KNIGHT: Do not tremble, Princess. I and my trusty sword will protect you.

PRINCESS: *Laughs unkindly.* You're the only one who's trembling. That sword's too big if you ask me. I've told you, I can look after myself. We're taught self-defence at school, nowadays, you know. *The Princess lunges towards the Knight, hands held high in front of her. She does a karate chop in the air. "Ha . . . Ha . . . Ha. SO!"*

(Sandra isn't ready for this, she is caught off guard and falls down. She has to be helped to her feet. Now, she is really mad and she means business.)

KNIGHT: Look here! Princess or no Princess, I have come to fight this Dragon. Why don't you hide yourself behind a tree while I dispose of him?

PRINCESS: Just how do you plan to do that?

KNIGHT: First, I will lure the beast out of his cave. Then I will challenge him to three days and nights of mortal combat. *The Knight performs a fast and fierce mime, which finishes with her hacking off the imaginary Dragon's head and carrying it, still dripping, to the Princess's feet.* In the end honour and bravery will prevail and I shall lay its ugly head at your dainty feet.

PRINCESS: You'd better not. I don't like blood and violence. If you ask me, it's a lot of fuss about nothing. It's only a Dragon.

KNIGHT: What do you mean, "*only* a Dragon?"

PRINCESS: Well, they're a bit pathetic, really. I mean, they can't go on eating Princesses. Girls won't put up with that kind of thing any more. Dragons'll be extinct in no time. They're a dying breed, like you lot. Knights – who needs them?"

KNIGHT: I can't listen to all this rubbish. I have a job to do. *The Knight takes a long rope from her horse. She gives one end to the Princess, and she takes her penknife away from her*. Please hold this.

The Knight races round the tree, holding the other end of the rope, until the Princess is securely tied.

PRINCESS: Hey, you can't do this to me. I'm a Princess. Knights are supposed to free Princesses, not tie them up. Didn't they teach you that at Knight School?

KNIGHT: Princesses usually know their place. Now keep quiet or I may have to gag you as well.

PRINCESS: Just you dare!

(This was clearly not agreed in rehearsals. It's a little extra idea of Sandra's to keep Jane quiet.)

The Knight approaches the cave. She throws her gauntlet, far into it. ("OOhya! That hurt!" can be faintly heard, followed by Cheryl's "Shshsh!")

KNIGHT: I, St Georgina, Knight of the Round Table, challenge you, Damselslayer, to come out and face me like a Dragon.

There are a few bad-tempered roars, "HRHR-HROW! HRHRHROW!"

KNIGHT: Come out and fight, you coward, instead
of hiding in there like a . . . MOUSE!

An offended roar is heard, "HRHRAARRUGH".
*The Knight peers into the cave, but still no Dragon
appears.*

(Jo doesn't recognize some of these lines. She has no
idea when she should come on. She is thoroughly
bored with waiting and limbering up, off-stage. She
decides now is as good a time as any. She makes her
entrance.)

*There is a clap of thunder (Cheryl bangs a metal tray
with a spoon), a flash of lightning (well, a bicycle lamp,
actually) and a drum-roll. A Witch appears, doing a
series of cartwheels across the stage. These are followed
by a backwards flip and finally a handstand. She has a
black cloak, tucked in the legs of her leotard. She is
wearing black tights and football boots. She peers
around and cackles nastily.*

WITCH: Haahaahaaaa. This looks like the place.
Now, who are you, may I ask?

PRINCESS: No, you may not. We were here first.

KNIGHT: We'll ask the questions. Who are you?

WITCH: I am Wilhelmina, Witch of the Woods. I have come in search of a despicable Dragon, which, I am told, lives in these parts.

PRINCESS: Well, you can join the queue and I'm first.

KNIGHT: What do *you* want with him?

WITCH: Hahahahaaa. *While she speaks the Witch does a series of leaps and spins.* (Sandra says it makes her look like someone having a fit.) I want to use him for my spells. I want his claws, and his blood, and his Dragon's Fire. And I want the tip of his terrible tail.

PRINCESS: Tchch. Not you as well. She wants to hack his head off, and now you want to chop him up and boil him in a cauldron. I should report you both to the R.S.P.C.D.

WITCH: Keep quiet, you, or I may lose my temper. I don't like Princesses.

175

(Jane sticks out her tongue. She's tired of being told to keep quiet.)

KNIGHT: You will have to take your turn, Madam. I have already challenged this Dragon. You'd better leave this job to the expert.

WITCH: *Cackles rudely*. You armour-plated idiot. This is my Dragon, now. Make another move and it may be your last. *The Witch points a finger at the Knight, like a loaded gun.*

KNIGHT: Now look here . . .

The Knight steps forward, threatening the Witch with her sword. The Witch jabs a bony finger at her. The Knight stops dead, apparently stuck to the spot.

KNIGHT: Let me go, you wizened old crone.

WITCH: Flattery will get you nowhere. *She cackles in triumph, while doing cartwheels around her victim.* Pretty clever trick, huh? Be careful, or next time I may turn you into a toad.

PRINCESS: That might be an improvement.

WITCH: And the same goes for you.

(Sandra and Jane pull an unpleasant face at each other. Now they are both out of action.)

The Witch makes her spell. This involves plenty of acrobatics.

(Jo would have liked a lot more, but Sandra complained that people had come to see some acting, not a gymnastics display.) *She finishes at the mouth of the cave and throws in a handful of imaginary powder. The Dragon roars,* "UGHGHHHHHHHRRRR-OOOWWWWWWWWGHGHGHGHGH-GHGHGH!" *The noise is deafening. The Witch retreats behind a tree, until it dies down.*

Just then a young woman sprints out of the woods. She turns around three times and then stands before them. She is wearing a strange costume, red, yellow and blue. Her entrance is accompanied by the "Wonder Woman" theme tune.

WITCH: And who are you supposed to be?

W.W.: *Sings*. My name is . . . "Wonder Woman."

Humming the Wonder Woman tune, she does several turns and wards off imaginary bullets with her wrist bands.

WITCH: Wonder Woman. Are you kidding?

W.W.: Wonder Woman is a real heroine. She is beautiful, wise, swift and strong. She is sworn to overcome evil, wherever it occurs.

WITCH: Then, why are you wearing that ridiculous outfit?

W.W.: This is part of my magic.

WITCH: So, you're a Witch really.

W.W.: I'm not a Witch, I'm an Amazon.

Wonder Woman demonstrates her powers. She fells a (cardboard) tree with one blow. She spins her crown across the clearing, to the Princess, who catches it and puts it on. She picks up the Witch and swings her above her head (well, almost clear of the ground).

WITCH: Hey, put me down. You can't do this to me. I'm Wilhelmina, Witch of the Woods.

W.W.: *She dusts off her hands.* Now perhaps you'd better tell me what's going on.

KNIGHT: We were here first. We'll ask the questions.

PRINCESS: Yeah, what are you doing here?

W.W.: I was visiting my mother, on Paradise Island, when I received a message, via Mental Radio. "England is under attack. Suspect extra-terrestrial terror. Lose no time. Go there at once." And so I flew straight here. For all we know, the whole Universe may be in danger.

A low rumbling is heard, in the depths of the cave. RRAAAARRRRGHGH. (It sounds as if the Dragon is getting hungry, or has fallen asleep and is snoring.)

W.W.: Merciful Minerva. You'd better leave this to me.

Wonder Woman prepares to do battle.

PRINCESS: But it's only a Dragon. I don't know what all the fuss is about.

KNIGHT: Why don't you go and find some aliens to wrestle with?

WITCH: Everything is under control, my control! Go away before I turn you into an extra-terrestrial toad.

The Witch points her finger at Wonder Woman. Wonder Woman takes out her golden lasso and, before the Witch can do a double back-flip, she has tied her to a tree. Now the Princess and the Witch are securely tied up and the Knight is rooted to the spot.

WITCH: You'll regret this, you under-dressed Amazon. You'll never capture the Dragon without me. Listen, we could do a deal. My magic and your muscle, we could take over the world. We could call ourselves, "Wonder Witches". There'd be no stopping us.

Wonder Woman leaps up on to the cave. With her bare fingers, she tries to break open the solid rock. The Dragon roars, "HRHRHRAAARRRGHGH-GH!" The cave shudders. Wonder Woman is thrown down, into the clearing. This is the cue for Dr Her's entrance. She appears, behind a stage-block, which she

pushes on. It is decorated, to look like a telephone box.
Dr Her steps out, dressed in a black suit and a top hat.

W.W.: Suffering Sappho! Who are you?

OTHERS: Yes, who are you?

DR HER: Permit me to introduce myself. Doctor Her, Scientist and Astral Traveller. I have just arrived in my time-capsule. I call her, "TARDHER". Can I be of any assistance to you?

All the others talk at the same time.

PRINCESS: Set me free, will you!'

KNIGHT: If you would free me, Doctor, I would soon see off this Dragon. Knights are trained for this kind of work.

WITCH: Get me out of here. *She stamps her foot.* This is my Dragon!

W.W.: If you would please assist me, Doctor . . .

DR HER: *Puts up her hands.* Silence, please. Together we can resolve these difficulties. Every problem has a solution, if we use our intelligence. Each of us wants to defeat the Dragon, correct?

They all mutter, "Yes", "Mmmmmm".

DR HER: Then why fight between ourselves? We should combine our strength and energy to combat the enemy.

PRINCESS: You mean we should join together?

DR HER: Exactly my point. Remember, "Girls should always stick together." For this job we need "The Girls' Gang".

Wonder Woman unties the Witch, who frees the Knight from her spell, who unties the Princess from the tree. The girls take off part of their costumes. Underneath they are wearing the letters "G.G." on their T-shirts. They gather round Cheryl and move to the front of the stage. They lower their voices, as if they are letting the audience in on a secret.

CHERYL: Now, let us consider the problem. In the cave we have a Dragon. *The others nod.*

The Dragon won't come out. *The others shake their heads.*

So, how can we tempt him out? *The others look puzzled.* What do Dragons like?

JANE: Princesses. But we tried that, it didn't work.

CHERYL: What kind of Princesses do Dragons like?

SANDRA: Weeping and wailing Princesses?

JO: Tied to a tree?

CHERYL: Exactly.

The Girls' Gang turn to the audience. "Shall we try it?" they ask. "Yes!!!" shouts the audience. Jane stands in front of a tree, hands behind her back. Sandra and Cheryl climb on top of the cave. Cheryl is carrying something rolled up in her hand. Louise and Jo hide behind the cave.

"Oh, help! Help! Save me," cries Jane.

This is the agreed cue for Ralph's long-awaited entrance. "About time," he thinks to himself. He is stiff from crouching and he has a sore throat. The enormous mask the girls have made for him is like a hot-house. He has to keep lifting it up to cool off. But now is his moment of glory. He doesn't plan to waste it. He staggers to the mouth of the cave, growling, "RRAARRGH!" He stands there to give the audience time to appreciate his magnificent appearance, before he launches his attack.

Cheryl and Sandra are stretching out a huge net. They point to Ralph, as if to say, "Shall we?"

"Yes!!!" yell the audience. Some of them also shout, "Behind you!" and "Look out!" They jab their fingers at Ralph.

"They certainly seem to be excited," he thinks. "Everyone is shouting. You'd think it was a rotten pantomime." But inside the mask, Ralph can't really make out *what* they are saying.

"Oh, help! Help! Save me . . ." cries Jane. Ralph lurches towards her, arms outstretched.

"QUICK . . . NOW!" she calls.

Cheryl and Sandra drop the net. It falls over him. Ralph is caught like a giant fly. He can't make out what is happening. Next, Jo does a rugby tackle, which fells him to the ground. Ralph struggles. He is totally unable to see what is going on. He wraps himself even tighter in the net. All five girls drop to the floor. They roll Ralph up, like a carpet. They stand around him, hands clasped above their heads.

They are the champions. Each girl has a foot on him. This is the final humiliation, he thinks. But the girls haven't finished yet. The five Amazons lift Ralph, struggling, up on to their shoulders. Then they begin a lap of honour around the stage, humming a marching tune. They sing, "Girls are the greatest".

The clapping is deafening. Everyone is cheering, even Mr Mills. Ralph thinks he must be going mad. This wasn't supposed to happen. Nobody said anything about this to him. The girls swing Ralph back and forth and pretend they might throw him into the audience. "Shall we? Shall we?" they ask.

"Yes!!!" cries the audience. There seems to be no limit to their heartlessness. They could cheerfully have watched whole families of Christians being sacrificed to the lions. But now, the girls have had their revenge. Ralph is heavy and they lower their prize gently to the floor. Despite Ralph's kicking, they manage to free him. They rush back beyond his reach. Ralph lashes out like a blind man. He lifts off the mask. His face is red and puffed up. He takes a deep breath and grits his teeth, ready for action.

But then, he looks out and sees the rest of the class, cheering and stamping and whistling. He realizes that this is all for him. He smiles and takes several bows. They call for "More!" He doesn't want to disappoint his audience. He gives them a final, stupendous roar. "HHHRRRROOOO-WWWWWWWWWGHGHGHGH!"

He pretends to savage the girls, who run off in genuine terror.

The play is over. The girls' gang and Ralph Raven take a total of ten curtain calls. The six of them are at last on the same side, players together. Sandra is so excited, she gives Ralph a spontaneous hug.

"You're a good sport," she says. Ralph pushes her away.

"Get off!" he says. He's had enough to put up with this afternoon, without that. The class invade the stage, like football supporters. They clap Ralph on the back. They vote him "Man of the Match".

Mr Mills watched the play spell-bound. It had been totally unexpected. These girls never ceased to amaze him. But the most puzzling question was, how had they ever persuaded Ralph to go along with it? The ending looked as if even he hadn't expected what was coming. Knowing the girls' gang, he almost believed that. He could begin to see how, one day, they really might take over the world.

Tomorrow, Year 6 would be leaving him. In a few

weeks' time they would start at the High School. He had just finished writing their record cards. He wondered, with a twinge of guilt, whether he ought to have warned the High School teachers about these girls. But then he thought to himself, "Teachers deserve their summer holiday. Why spoil it for them? They'll find out, soon enough."

Fireballs from Hell

by Rose Impey

Sam, Jamie and Luke have a band called
FIREBALLS FROM HELL, or do they? It's
a brilliant idea, but it does seem to require
rather a lot of work putting it together, and an
astonishing amount of things they haven't got
– instruments, transport, a demo tape,
somewhere to practise, backing – *backing*?
Does that mean girls? Aagh!

Girls could be all right, provided they
weren't sisters or the dreaded Victoria
Topping, but you had to be careful who you
admitted it to. Are girls genuinely needed for
the band, or are they suddenly becoming more
interesting anyway? Luke sometimes thinks
so, Jamie thinks he thinks so (but not without
blushing), Sam has distinct reservations.

Find out what happens for yourself!

£3.50

Order Form

To order direct from the publishers, just make a list of the titles you want and fill in the form below:

Name ....

Address ....

....

....

Send to: Dept 6, HarperCollins Publishers Ltd, Westerhill Road, Bishopbriggs, Glasgow G64 2QT.

Please enclose a cheque or postal order to the value of the cover price, plus:

UK & BFPO: Add £1.00 for the first book, and 25p per copy for each addition book ordered.

Overseas and Eire: Add £2.95 service charge. Books will be sent by surface mail but quotes for airmail despatch will be given on request.

A 24-hour telephone ordering service is avail-able to Visa and Access card holders: 041-772 2281